Broken

A Fling,Sports,Workplace,Billionaire Romance

Heart of Stone
Book 1

Chiquita Dennie

304 Publishing Company

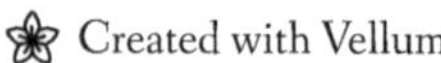 Created with Vellum

This book is dedicated to my family, especially (Rhonda Dennie, Grandma, and Aunt Marcia) for always believing in me. Also, I want to shout out my big Brent Dennie, JD, Christopher, Lil James, Jazzypoo, my sisters, and best friends from Memphis: Nita, San, Reese, Jennifer, LA besties Tavi & Tiffany for always supporting me. Shout out to all of my cousins, nieces, and nephews.

Author Inspiration

"Never allow anyone to steal your joy. It doesn't matter how many times someone says you can't do something. Invest in yourself—even if it's just writing down what your goals and plans are. Starting small can lead to bigger things."

—Chiquita Dennie

Latest Releases from Chiquita Dennie

The Early Years-A Prequel Short Story
    Struck in Love 1, 2, 3,4,5
    Heart of Stone, Book 1 (Emery & Jackson)
    Heart Of Stone Book 1.5 Emery &Jackson A Valentine's Day Short
    Janice and Carlo: Captivated By His Love
    Heart of Stone, Book 2 (Jordan and Damon)
    Temptation
    Heart of Stone, Book 3 (Angela and Brent)
    Bottoms Up Heart of Stone, Book 3.5(Jessica and Joseph Short
    Cocky Catcher
    Bossy Billionaire
    Love Shorts:A Collection of Short Stories
    Stolen Fuertes Mafia Cartel Book 1
    Saved Fuertes Mafia Cartel Book 2
    Exposed (Salvation Society Novel)
    Betrayal Fuertes Mafia Cartel Book 3
    Refuel(A Driven World Novel)
    Pressure(A Driven World Novel)

Disclaimer

This work of fiction contains strong language and explicit sexual content and is only intended for mature readers. This story may contain unconventional situations, language, and sexual encounters that may offend some readers.I would recommend another book. This book is for mature readers (18+).

Introduction

Are you signed up for my newsletter?

Join today and find out all the latest in new releases, contests, giveaways, sneak peeks and more.
www.chiquitadennie.com

Synopsis

He was just supposed to be a one-night stand.

Emery is determined to live a life with no strings attached. She'd rather have one-night stands then make things complicated with boyfriends or relationships. She's been there and done that and it didn't end well.

Unfortunately for her, her no strings attached date from last night just became a very big complication for her.

She was meant to be my forever.

Jackson has finally found someone that he can't stop thinking about. He knows that Emery has reservations and that she's built up walls around herself but he's determined to break through them.

When he finds out that Emery's ex-fiancé has come back into her life, he starts to have doubts.

Can a one-night stand lead to something more for these two?

Chapter One

Emery

The beeping of the hospital monitor used to drive me crazy when I was younger and visited my grandfather as he battled cancer. Every time we came for a visit, I'd somehow get lost in counting the beeps. Lately, we'd come for my grandmother because of her high blood pressure. A few days ago, I would have never imagined the way my life would turn out since Anthony and I broke up.

"Emery, Emery honey!" Mom called out.

"Oh Lord, Elisabeth, my grandchild done gone into shock," Granny stated.

"Ma, she's not in shock," Elisabeth said.

"Hush. Yes, she is or what they call it, now turned out."

"Huh?" I answered.

"Momma, what do you know about turning out?" Mom questioned.

"Sorry, I just zoned out for a second," I responded.

"Zoned out, turned out. At the end of the day, it's all the same in my book."

"Emery, pass me my purse."

"Oh sure, here you go."

"I'm going downstairs to grab something to eat. You want anything?"

"I'm fine."

"Grab me a burger and fries," Granny answered.

"Momma, you're in the hospital for high cholesterol and blood pressure. I'm not getting you a burger and fries."

Granny waved Mom off and rolled her eyes.

"Emery, your mother's a hater."

Laughing at her statement, my mother shook her head in disbelief.

"Now that your mother's gone, tell me what's really going on."

Walking closer to her bed, I tilted my head on her shoulder. She massaged my hand and kissed my cheek.

"Honey, you can lie to your parents and even to your friends but not to Granny, so spill the beans before your nosy momma gets back."

"Granny, how can you call her nosy when you're trying to get in my business?"

She folded her arms and tapped me on the forehead. "Hush, child. I'm your grandmother; we can do that. Now spill the tea."

Fiddling with my earrings and avoiding eye contact, we all knew she would get the truth out of us at one point with just narrowing her eyes. All the grandkids and even my mom and dad fell into her spell of never lying; the truth was easier than covering up a lie.

"Emery, I have all the time in the world. Now either you tell me, or I go ask your mother."

"Granny, it's not that serious. Anthony and I broke up."

"About damn time!"

Shocked at her words, I cowered in the corner of her hospital bed, running a hand down my face and blowing out a breathy sigh.

"Listen, I know you're friends with his sister. I like the boy, but as far as boyfriend material? Ummm... I'd pass."

"He cheated with Teresa."

"What now?"

"I caught him in bed with Teresa."

"Teresa, your best friend Teresa?"

"Yep."

Granny jumped out of bed and walked over to the drawer to remove her clothes. I jumped up and drew nearer.

"What are you doing?"

Taking the clothes out of her hands. I placed them back down and pulled her back to the bed.

"We about to take care of her. Don't nobody hurt my baby and get away with it. That hussy will get her ass kicked."

Waving her off, I placed her back in the bed right as Mom walked back inside. "You can't talk like that. Besides, I'm handling it."

"Let me call Angela, and we gonna ride out tonight. Forget Jordan, she may lie and hide with Teresa."

"Oh my God! Granny, leave Jordan and Angela out of this. Just get some rest for me, please. You'll get your blood pressure up."

Mom placed the food tray down on the bedside counter and pulled out a salad and fruit mix for Granny.

"What the hell is that?" Granny shrieked.

"Your dinner, Momma."

"Elisabeth, now I know you ain't that damn prissy that you can't get me real food besides some damn salad. My husband likes me with meat on my bones."

"Just eat your food so we can get out of here."

Chuckling at the exchange, I decided to leave for the night and meet up with Angela and Jordan.

"Since you're back, Mom, I'm going to take off and meet Angela for dinner and drinks."

Kissing Granny on her forehead, and Mom on her cheek, I headed toward the door right as Granny made a comment.

"Emery, don't forget I still got friends in Hamilton Projects. Let Teresa know she gonna see me."

"Okay, Granny, love you!" I bellowed out.

Chapter Two

Emery

Heading to dinner with my two best friends, I realized I never introduced myself. I'm Emery Stone born and raised in New York City. I'm twenty-six years old, African American, five-foot-six with coffee-brown skin, heart-shaped face, button nose, shoulder-length curly hair, and an hourglass figure or as to society's standards of being curvy. An account executive at Townsend Advertising Firm owned by one of my best friends Brent Townsend.

Arriving at the restaurant, my phone vibrated in my purse. A message from Anthony appeared.

Anthony: Emery, please pick up the phone.

Me: Fuck U

Anthony: I want us to still be friends

Me: That's funny seeing as how you hated for me to have guy friends. Anthony, leave me alone and go tend to your pregnant girlfriend.

Anthony: We can figure this out.

I shut my phone down and massaged my temple from

Anthony's constant aggravation. I tossed it back into my purse and stepped out of my car.

"Well, look what the cat dragged in. Emery Stone. I guess you win the bet, Jordan. She showed up tonight." Angela threw her head back in laughter.

Flashing my middle finger at her, I bypassed them both to enter Sybil's, a Southern cuisine restaurant.

"Boo, you know she didn't mean it. Tell her you're sorry, Angela," Jordan demanded.

"She knows I'm just joking. Besides, a little fun will help distract from you know who."

Jordan and I avoided eye contact, and I walked forward to the hostess booth.

"How many in your party?"

"Three please. Can we have a booth in the corner?"

The hostess nodded and gestured with a wave of her hand for us to follow her to our seats. Walking through the restaurant, I felt someone staring at me and, out of the corner of my eye, I saw a tall African American man with deep dark-chocolate skin, full lips, and what looked like ripped muscles in his tailored suit.

I just recently broke up with my cheating ex-boyfriend Anthony Davis, who happened to be the big brother of my best friend Jordan Davis. Looking down at my outfit, I noticed the cut of the skirt hugging my wide hips and my thick thighs poking out. My large DD breasts were still sitting up nicely, even though sometimes, I complained about getting a reduction.

"Ouch!"

Angela and Jordan ran into the back of me.

"Damn, Emery, pay attention. What has you frozen in your tracks?"

"Nothing, nothing, let's go eat."

"I think it has something to do with that fine black man over at that table."

Pulling Angela and Jordan toward our booth, I scrambled to sit down out of sight as my heart nearly stopped, and my body ached with need. The panties I wore were ruined from my arousal from the guy that just stole my breath away.

"Your waiter will be right with you."

"Thanks. Emery, are you okay? You look a little flushed," Jordan asked.

"Yes, I just need some water."

"Oh, look. Brent's here eating with that guy you were staring at, Emery."

"I wasn't staring at anyone, Jordan," I told her.

Turning my head, I noticed the gentleman pointing at our table and Brent looking over at us and smiling. He stood and walked over to our table with mystery man behind him.

"Damnit," I muttered out.

"Someone's nervous," Angela whispered, delighted.

Throwing my napkin at her playfulness, I flipped her the middle finger and fixed myself up before Brent approached with his guest. Why I was doing all that, I couldn't say. I was still heartbroken over Anthony's lying and cheating.

"Well, if it isn't my best account executive, Emery Stone, out to dinner with her two best friends, Jordan Davis and Angela Jones."

"Hi, Brent."

"Don't get shy now. What's up, Big Head, and who's your friend?" Angela asked.

Angela had me in disbelief with my mouth agape at

her words. Watching her snicker with Jordan and Brent, the mystery guy continued to stare at me.

"Ignore her, Brent. Hi, I'm Jordan Davis, and this is Angela Jones and from the heat radiating off you two, this is Emery Stone," Jordan shook mystery guy's hand.

"This is Jackson Pierce, an old friend. Jackson's my boy from back home. We grew up together and eventually, we went to separate schools and met back up a few years ago after his divorce."

Hearing Brent say Jackson was divorced gave me butterflies in my stomach.

"Pleased to meet you, Emery Stone." Jackson extended his hand for me to grab. Something inside me hesitated for a second.

"Ni... Nice to meet you as well, Jackson," I stuttered out.

He smiled at my misstep and continued holding my hand and rubbing his fingers against my knuckles. I arched my brow and caught the entire table watching us.

"Are you going to let my hand go?" I asked.

Jackson bit down on his lower lip and raised my hand to his lips, placing a soft kiss on the back. I rose fast out of the booth. The throbbing between my thighs rose, and I felt the sexual heat between us. Thinking clearly and remembering we were in front of other people, I tried to focus on something else before ending up on my back with my legs wrapped around his thick, strong thighs. God wouldn't be that cruel and let this gorgeous guy walk around with a little dick.

"I wasn't planning on it, sweetness."

"Oh, I like you, Jackson. Do you have a brother or an uncle by chance?" Angela blurted out.

Brent narrowed his eyes at Angela, and she shrugged

her shoulders in exasperation. *What's going on between those two?*

"Angela, don't get your feelings hurt. I suggest you keep your eyes on that menu before you get in trouble."

Jordan and I paused at Brent chastising Angela in public. They'd always had a fiery friendship and with me working for him and her as my best friend, I often found her coming to my job to hang out. I couldn't have a screaming match.

"Brent, you're not my daddy, boyfriend, husband, or boss. Your suggestions are not needed this way. Now, Jackson, as I was saying," Angela stated.

Jackson patted Brent on the back and calmed him down as he inched closer to Angela.

"How about we just order dinner? Brent, would you like to join us?" Jordan suggested.

"Actually, we're meeting some guests tonight. Thanks anyway, Jordan. I'll see you tomorrow, Emery."

"Bye, Brent," Jordan and I replied.

He walked away, ignoring Angela. She sat with her arms crossed and lips turned up in a pout.

"Is there something I should know about Angela Jones?"

"No."

"Please tell me you're not sleeping with Brent."

"No, I'm not."

Sitting back down in my seat, I leaned back and relaxed from the built-up tension in the room.

"I mean if you don't count last Christmas, Super Bowl Weekend, and Jordan's baby shower."

"Bitch, you slept with him at my baby shower! Are you crazy?" Jordan screamed.

"What? Don't act like you tramps don't have an itch that needs scratching every blue moon."

"Angela, there's a difference between an itch and a fuck buddy," Jordan said.

"Are you and Brent in a relationship?"

"Hell, no. We mutually decided to keep what we have just between us. So, don't you go running your mouth, Emery Stone. Brent and I are friends, and occasionally, we sleep together."

"So, he sleeps with other women, and you're okay with that?" Jordan asked.

"Yep, just like I sleep with other men," Angela replied.

"Well, he may be getting lucky tonight. The women are throwing themselves at him right now. He's pulling his phone out. Bet he comes in late tomorrow, Emery," Jordan answered.

Angela stood out of her seat, knocking her water over the table. She shrieked as it splashed onto her dress.

"That bastard," Angela groaned.

"I thought you weren't in a relationship, Angela?"

"We aren't. He can get any slut's phone number he wants. I mean if he wants to catch a disease, then by all means, get her number. She looks like a man anyway," Angela said.

We all burst into laughter and asked the waiter to bring another glass of water and some wine to our table.

"So, Emery, how is Granny doing?" Jordan asked.

I picked around the olives in the arugula salad. Food had always been a weakness. Lately, I'd started this new vegan lifestyle change. Not sure it would last long because I loved cheese too much.

"I just left her with my mom earlier. Her blood pressure and cholesterol are up. You know Granny Lynn doesn't stay on top of her health. She loves three things in this world besides her family: soul food, cigarettes, and rum and Coke."

"That's true. I remember at the last family dinner, she made this mac and cheese that stuck with me for days after," Angela responded.

"For what it's worth, she still looks good for a woman in her seventies, I must say. Her shape is bananas, probably why Jackson Pierce hasn't taken his eyes off you, Emery, since we've sat down," Jordan told her.

"If you don't want him, Emery, I'll take him off your hands. Add to my roster of fun," Angela smirked jokingly.

Turning around slowly and trying to play off Angela's comment, I caught Jackson staring right at me. I smiled back and turned around with Angela and Jordan peering deviously.

"What?"

We all cracked up laughing, and Jordan picked up her fork and continued eating her pasta salad.

"How's the little man doing, Jordan?"

"Good, my baby is growing so fast. I still can't believe it's been over two years since I lost Devin. Every day is a struggle with raising him as a single mother. Without my parents and Anthony, I wouldn't know where I'd end up."

"We all miss him. Devin couldn't wait to be a father, and you're an amazing mother."

"Do you think it's time to get back in the dating world?" Angela asked.

Wiping the tears from her eyes with a napkin, Jordan shook off Angela's statement.

"I'm not ready. Besides, DJ takes up all my time, along with work as a teacher."

Grabbing and squeezing her hand to comfort her, all three of us wiped our eyes before the tears fell.

"Jordan, you got me out here being soft and shit. I need a drink," Angela replied.

"Angela, you drink no matter if you're happy, sad, horny, or stuck in a winter thunderstorm. Don't blame me for you being an alcoholic," Jordan grumbled as she drank from her water glass.

Listening to them bicker reminded me of Teresa and my relationship before the cheating. We stayed in each other's business and supported one another no matter what. Knowing she'd been shady going behind my back with Anthony all this time had me wondering if he ever tried anything with Angela.

"Emery, Emery!" Jordan snapped loudly.

"Huh?"

"Are you okay?"

"Yeah, why do you ask?"

"You just zoned out on us again. Is something wrong?"

"No, I'm fine. Just thinking about my grandmother and—"

"Please don't bring up Anthony's sorry, lying, cheating ass."

"Well damn, tell me how you feel about my brother."

"I just did." Angela shrugged her shoulders nonchalantly.

Clapping my hands to gain both of their attention, a figure walked up to our table before I could speak.

"Excuse me, ladies. Do you mind if I steal Miss Stone away for a second?" Jackson asked.

He wrapped his hand around my elbow and smoothly pulled me out of my seat.

"Well damn, excuse us, Mr. Pierce. She's all yours for the night. Just have her back by tomorrow for work," Angela mocked jokingly.

Jackson led me away from the table, and I grabbed my purse before it was left behind. Walking outside, I noticed we were headed to his car.

"Ummm, I'm not leaving with you."

"Emery, you and I both know that before the end of the night, I'm going to have you tied and twisted with you screaming my name. The real question is my place or yours?" Jackson demanded.

Swallowing the want of having him ravish me in the parking lot, I looked back at the restaurant for Angela or Jordan popping out to stop me.

"How about a hotel room?"

"Lead the way, sweetness."

Chapter Three

Jackson

Sitting inside Sybil's, something told me to look up. The woman who walked through the door took my breath away. I was waiting on my friend Brent to come back from a telephone call when an aroma passed by me with a lingering smell of peaches. I couldn't take my eyes off her. She walked right past my table. I stood around six foot three in height with smooth chocolate-brown skin, six-pack abs, broad shoulders, small dimples on each cheek, and a short goatee.

From that moment on, I decided she would be mine. When Brent came back inside, and I pointed her out, he made it known that she was off limits. At first, when Brent said it, every muscle in my body tensed, and my blood boiled. He noticed my rage with my fist opening and closing and eyes narrowing. Quickly, he informed me that Emery not only worked for him but also just got out of a relationship with a friend of his who cheated on her with her best friend.

Now here we were, both walking into the W Hotel, that I often used when entertaining clients, or I needed female companionship. They made sure everything was to my liking when I visited. It didn't hurt that the owners were lifelong ticket holders at our races.

Before I slid the key into the door, Emery reached her small, dainty, soft hand around my neck and leaned her heaving breasts against my chest. We kissed, first lightly, then more urgently, with my tongue in her mouth. Her hips tilted against me, her entire body sending a message there was no denying. Both fighting for dominance that neither would relinquish.

Her tongue fluttered against my lips, and I ran my hands through the softness of her hair. It was like we were two high school kids trying to become one, not knowing where I started and she ended.

She nibbled at *my* ear and bottom lip. Smoothing her fingertips down my chest, sighing and whispering, "I need you now." Backing her up against the bedroom door, we both twisted the knob to the bedroom and walked inside, not leaving any space between us. I opened the curtains and kept the lights turned off, silently standing there as she slowly peeled off her clothing.

Lying back onto the bed, she propped herself onto her elbows and watched as I pulled off her shoes one by one. Massaging, then kissing, each toe, and hearing her low moans come from her plump, beautiful lips made the anticipation even higher. Squeezing and biting delicately.

Emery helped unbutton my shirt, then eased my briefs over my hips, brushing the length of my cock with her palm before taking me entirely in her mouth. I sighed, eyes shut, thinking about how unbelievably good it felt, when Emery gave a throaty moan, then rolled her mouth from base to tip and whispered, "Look at me."

I saw that she had her eyes open, locked on me, as she

hollowed her cheeks and slid me all the way down. I wondered how dumb Anthony was to cheat on someone like her. At the same time, I needed to make sure she never did this with anyone else. After tonight, she was mine.

"What?" Emery asked.

"Shh," I said, pulling her up, so we were face to face again. I slid my hands between her legs, positioning my index finger and thumb in her beautiful, tight pussy. She nuzzled against me, kissing my neck and nibbling on my earlobe.

"Ooh," she whispered. "Yes! Oh, oh, oh," she sighed, as I worked a finger against the slick walls. I watched her squeeze her eyes shut as she clamped her thighs against my wrist and arched her back. Squirming before she froze, all the muscles in her legs and belly tensed and quivered, as I felt her contract against my fingers.

Before she could recover, I rolled her onto her back and slipped inside her. I didn't move as I took in her wet, tight, and warm mound, trying to hold onto the little bit of composure I had left before releasing and turning into a minuteman. I thought of anything dealing with politics, sports, or the last race we lost to distract me from coming too early.

"Jackson!"

"Yes, sweetness?"

"Please..."

Leaning over to lay soft, gentle kisses on her forehead and lips, I thrusted at an even pace. I needed to savor this moment.

"Mmmm... you feel so good," Emery whispered.

"You do too, sweetness," I groaned into her ear as I

sped up, pounding into her wetness. Falling deeper into her canal.

Grabbing her left leg around my waist and placing her right one against my shoulder, I was able to delve deeper into her.

"Arghh... God wait!"

Seeing the tears in her eyes, I kissed the pain and pleasure away as best as I could.

"I've waited long enough for you."

She opened her eyes, and we both stared at each other as I continued to pull as she pushed her hand against my lower stomach.

"Move your hand, sweetness."

Emery shook her head. I smirked and released her left leg. Grabbing her hands, I ravaged her neck, then leaned to her chest to lick and nuzzle her breasts. After placing on a condom, my goal was to make sure I left a mark, so she'd never forget our time together.

"Shit, Emery... Fuck."

I picked up the pace as the headboard hit the wall. I felt my orgasm nearing and pulled out, stroking my dick faster as she jumped up and took me into her mouth as she sucked the last of my seed from the condom.

"Arghhh... Fuck, sweetness!" I cried out.

Putting on another condom, I turned her on her side. Lifting her leg, I tapped my dick up and down her clit, teasing and watching the faces she made as she tried to push me away. Finally feeling like she had enough, I slowly eased back in.

"Fuck, Emery...You're so warm and tight, baby."

` I needed her to come at least once more with me.

"It's too much..." she moaned with her mouth gaped

open. I leaned over and bit her bottom lip and grabbed her chin, holding her in place as I plunged my tongue into her mouth. Trying to dominate every part of her body.

"Oh, God," she whispered, swiveling her hips in a way I knew would send me right over the edge. "Ughhh, wait. Sweetness, shittt..." I whispered.

Her heavy breathing increased as my thrusts slowed down. Wanting to be near, she wrapped her arms around my neck and tilted closer for a kiss. She took a deep, steady breath, and I was able to flip her over and lay her flat on her stomach. I plunged my tongue into her sweet, heavenly pussy and told her to ride my tongue the way she just pleased my dick.

She gasped and shut her eyes, and then neither of us could speak. She had one hand on the headboard, and the other slowly tightened around the sheets, grasping for anything that would help her escape.

"You feel so good," she whispered. I couldn't hold back any longer. I plunged inside her, deep into that maddening clutch, that heat. Emery moaned, pulling her hands away from the headboard and sheets. I tightened my hold on her with her arms behind her and leaned over with my chest to her back.

"Oh, baby," I gasped as she turned her head and put her lips against my ear, whispering my name over and over, like a song.

A few hours later, Emery was still in my arms, curled against my chest, and said, "I'll let you rest for a few hours before round two," in a joking tone with her hands balled into fists. She punched lightly at my chest, easing my arms around her. I ran my hands down her soft, coffee-brown skin as we drifted off to sleep.

I woke up, reaching out for her, and realized she was

no longer in bed. Getting up to check the bathroom and kitchen, all her things were missing. Chuckling to myself how I was the one who always left before the women woke.

"I guess Emery Stone's in for a chase."

Chapter Four

Emery

Stumbling off the elevator at work, I waved at my coworkers and walked toward my office. Noticing Brent's door closed, I headed over and knocked.

Hearing mumbling and moaning. I placed my ear against the door.

"Ummm, Big Daddy, don't stop," she moaned loudly.

"Shush, Angela... You know Barbara's nosy-ass will hear you," Brent replied.

"Gimme a kiss, and I promise not to talk back again."

"Brent, is Angela in there?" I whispered loudly.

"Shit, I told you to be quiet. Now she knows," Brent said.

"It's only Emery, and she won't tell. Now keep going, I'm almost there, baby."

"Angela, get your nasty ass out of there right now. Brent, open this door," I snapped in frustration.

Hearing scrambling in the room, after a few minutes, the door opened, and Angela walked out with her shirt inside out and a hickey on her neck.

"Are you two seriously doing this at work?"

"I just came by to ask Brent some marketing advice for the salon."

"Angela, do I look like boo-boo the fool to you?"

"Whatever, you can't talk anyway. I see that hickey on your neck. Who are you trying to fool?"

"What hickey?"

"Excuse me, ladies, but can you take this somewhere else? I have a meeting in a few minutes with a new client. Angela, the secret is out of the bag. Emery, we're dating," Brent said.

"No, we hang out from time to time. I don't belong to anyone," Angela smartly said.

Brent smacked her on the ass, and she scoffed and walked off toward my office.

"Is this going to be a problem for me?" I asked.

"Shit, I should ask you the same thing. That woman drives me crazy."

"You seem to keep going back, so obviously you like it."

Brent drew in a long breath and sighed as he shook his head back and forth.

"I've tried plenty of times to get her out of my system, Emery. She frustrates me with dating other guys and ignoring my calls when she sees I'm out with other women."

"You love her."

He chuckled and waved me off and opened his office door for me to walk inside.

"We have a meeting with a client this morning. The founder and CEO of Pierce NASCAR motors. I want you heading the account and bring Dominique in on it as well."

"Why her? You know we can't stand each other."

"Emery, please. For me, be nice."

Drinking the last of my coffee, I tossed the cup in his wastebasket and grabbed the files out of his hands.

"Sure thing, boss."

I turn to leave, but he called me back.

"Oh, Emery, you may want to put a little makeup on your neck, seeing as how we're in a professional setting."

"Umm..."

"No need to come up with an excuse. I know you're still recovering from your breakup with Anthony. Judgment-free zone here."

"I guess we both have stressful love affairs at the moment."

"Have you talked with him lately?"

"Don't."

"I'm on your side, Emery. We've almost come to blows over you."

"Thanks, Brent, but I'm a big girl. I can fight my own battles."

"I know. How is Granny Lynn doing? I called her last week about Sunday dinner, and she cursed me out, saying, *Boy, all you do is call me when you're hungry. Better find you a woman to cook for you since Angela's only good for doing hair and laying on her back.* I swear, Emery, Granny is crazy and needs a check."

We both burst into laughter. After leaving Brent's office, I walked over to my office and noticed the door open. Peeking inside, Angela sat behind my desk with her feet propped up, talking on my phone.

I closed the door behind me, laid the file folder on the desk, and kicked her feet down.

"Let me call you back, J. Grouchy just walked inside,

and you know how she is if she doesn't eat anything first thing in the morning."

"She'll call you back later, Jordan."

Pointing for her to get out of my seat, she raised and walked around my desk to sit in the chair.

"How was last night?"

"How about we talk about you and your little friendly visit with my boss?"

"Who? Brent?"

"Yes, Brent or shall I say Big Daddy."

"You're too grouchy this early in the morning. The dick must not have been that good."

"Angela, I swear you have a few screws loose. Anyway, the sex was fabulous if you must know. I still can't believe I had a one-night stand."

"Me neither. So, what was the sex like? Don't hold back on anything." Angela moved to my couch as I came around and sat next to her in the chair.

"He was so attentive, making sure my needs came first. I couldn't tell you how many orgasms I had, and the size was very pleasing."

"Ohh... I love a man with a big dick, especially if he can work it. Let me tell you about Brent."

"Uhmm... that's my cue to start working."

"What? I listened to you talk about your one-night stand."

"And what makes you think I want to hear about you sleeping with my friend and boss?"

Angela snorted at my comment and waved me off as Dominique appeared at my door.

"Morning, Emery. Are you ready for the meeting with the client?" Dominique asked as she glared at Angela.

Those two never got along because Angela always

said she flirted and tried to push up on Brent multiple times.

"Don't you knock?"

"Don't you have a job? Or is sitting around eating and braiding hair your job?" Dominique snapped sassily.

"All right, you two," I scolded them both with a disappointing glare.

"I have a client to meet, Emery. I'll call you later, and Doloris—"

Dominique swerved around fast and glared at Angela with her hands on her hips, tapping her feet. "My name is Dominique."

Angela waved her off as she walked out of my office.

"That's what I said. Anyway, talk later, Emery, and dinner's on you." Angela shut my door on her way out as I snickered at her comment toward Dominique.

Dominique rolled her eyes at Angela and turned back around, facing me.

"How can I help you, Dominique?" I sighed in irritation at her interruption.

"We have a meeting with a new client, and Brent sent me to get you."

"I know about the meeting. I don't need a babysitter, and it does say Executive VP-Advertising on my door." Gathering my notes and files, I picked up my black shawl that I purchased the other night, since I couldn't get home to change after the events of last night.

"We all know you're Brent's favorite. I don't need a reminder. I'm trying to score this deal, so I can keep my record solid. We don't need to work together. Just give me your files, and I'll handle everything, and as usual, you take credit." Dominique smirked as she walked out of my office. I followed her to the conference room.

Checking to see if I missed any messages from my mom, I noticed a text from Anthony.

Anthony: Em, please call me.

Emery: We have nothing to talk about.

"Watch where you're—"

Annoyed that Anthony was still trying to get back together, I replied and ended up bumping into the back of a very tall figure. I backed up and peered from the size fifteen Marc Jacob loafers up to the wide shoulders, broad smile, and full lips that sucked on my breasts for hours and hours, with long, thick hands that caressed my wide hips as he pumped into me at every angle, wearing a mischievous smile. Spacing out, I realized that I had slept with my new client last night.

"Emery, this is Jackson Pierce. You remember him from the restaurant," Brent informed me as he escorted all of us into the conference room.

Taking a deep breath, I shook Jackson's hand and then moved to the other side of the room to keep distance between us.

"Yes, I remember Mr. Pierce. Nice to see you again, sir."

"Please, call me Jackson."

"I prefer Mr. Pierce. Brent would have a fit if I didn't properly address his friend and client correctly."

"You're fine, Emery. Whatever Jackson needs, give it to him. Nothing is off limits," Brent said, and I stared into Jackson's eyes, and he winked at me. I picked up the glass of water in front of me and took a sip to distract myself from the throbbing ache between my legs.

"Jackson, I put Emery on your account because she's the best ad executive I have. I would personally oversee things normally—"

Jackson waved him off and unbuttoned his jacket as he sat straighter, folding his hands in front of him. I licked my lips in remembrance of the way he tasted in my mouth as I ran my tongue up and down his thick shaft.

"Emery! Emery!" Brent shouted my name and waved his hand in front of my face.

"Huh?"

"Where did you go? I was calling you," Brent said.

Shuffling the papers in front of me, I turned toward Dominique. She glared at me with her lip pouted out like a little kid throwing a tantrum.

"Sorry, I was thinking about the workload Dominique and I will have to split up."

"I can handle Mr. Pierce all by myself if Emery is too overwhelmed with other accounts." Dominique crossed her arms under her chest as her breasts spilled out of her shirt. Brent lingered at her DD boobs as I caught Jackson staring at me.

"I prefer to work with Emery one on one," Jackson said.

"What!" Dominique and I both yelled out at the same time.

"I don't think that's a good idea, Jackson. Emery has more than just you as a client, which is why I partnered her up with Dominique," Brent said as he walked around to the conference door to leave.

"Yeah, I agree with Brent, Mr. Pierce. You need more than one set of hands and eyes on your project. I'm known for having satisfied clients and account ratings," Dominique explained with a smirk on her face as she tossed her hair back and leaned in to show off her breasts more.

I rolled my eyes at her blatant flirtation in front of a client and our boss.

"I'd rather have Emery. Brent, you wouldn't mind, would you? I can throw in another year of advertising in our deal if I exclusively work with Emery."

Blinking repeatedly at his statements, I paused to wait and hear what Brent had to say.

"Emery can speak for herself. If her other accounts don't suffer, I'm fine with that. But keep Dominique on for the daily calls and meetings, and Emery can run things through her as a second lead," Brent replied and shook Jackson's hand. Watching Brent leave the office, I gulped the rest of my water down, thinking of a way to get out of this situation.

"Dominique, could you give Emery and I a minute alone?" Jackson asked.

"No," I said out in a rush.

Jackson and Dominique both looked at me. Dominique suspiciously and Jackson amusingly at my nervousness to be alone with him.

"Should I be worried?" Dominique asked.

I lowered my head and ran a hand across my forehead to gather my thoughts.

"I'm fine, Dominique. Give us a minute, and then we can start."

Dominique stood and put her skirt down, hoping to catch Jackson's eyes. Unbeknownst to her and Brent, I was the one he stared at for the last hour we'd been in this room. She left as Jackson and I played the staring game.

"Are you going to stare at me all day?" I asked.

He slowly stood, pulled his jacket down at the sleeves, licked his lips, and walked over to close the conference room door.

"We should leave that open."

Shaking his head, he came around the table to where I sat. He stopped in front of me as I turned in my seat with my legs crossed, cursing under my breath for wearing the same dress from last night. It showed off more than enough thighs.

He stared down and leaned over to look me directly in the face.

Chapter Five

Jackson

I was a very confident and determined man, growing up as the only child of Loretta and Charles Pierce. My father was the first black man to become a billionaire from oil in Texas. I grew up wanting to follow in his footsteps, fascinated with fast cars and making money. I graduated with a business degree, and a friend told me about how NASCAR was restructuring. I created Pierce Motors, a diverse team of drivers from not only the front seat but behind the scenes to the cockpit, office staff, janitors, and announcers.

We took off, and slowly I became the president of NASCAR over the entire division. Getting Emery Stone to see us as more than a one-night stand would be a challenge I planned on winning. Remembering her smell, taste, and cries of passion for me at the number of times I made her orgasm last night had my dick hard right now. Caressing my favorite spot on her body, her smooth hips, I picked her up out of her seat and placed her on top of the table.

"What are—"

I shushed her with a motion to be quiet, while opening her legs wider and stepping between to join our bodies. I could sense her arousal and nervousness at not knowing what I was about to do. The conference room was soundproofed with dark walls, and the only windows angled toward the traffic outside. Placing my hands on her hips, I soothingly placed a kiss underneath her ear.

"You look beautiful today," I said as I caressed her cheek and placed a second kiss under her ear.

Feeling her heat radiate off me had my balls wanting to burst out of my pants.

"You can't do this at my job. What happened last night was a one-time thing," Emery whispered lowly.

"You don't believe that, do you?"

Turning away from my body, she pushed me back, and I gave her space to gather her thoughts.

"I... I need for you to keep this professional, or I'll have someone else take over your account," Emery stuttered out.

"Okay."

"What?"

"I said okay. Keep it professional; we had a moment, and now it's over. I can work with you and keep things business as usual. Scout's honor."

"Good, good. First thing we need to do is come up with a strategy for the new season. Are you kicking off an exhibition race?" she asked, standing and gathering her paperwork.

"We are, and you should come."

"That's not necessary."

I opened the door for her to lead the way out.

"I think it is."

I held my hand up to stop her from arguing with me.

"Brent put you in charge of my account, correct?"

She rolled her eyes in annoyance at me. I licked my lips, remembering being between her sweet slick folds last night.

"Keep rolling your eyes like that, Emery, and they'll end up getting stuck."

"I... I..."

"Don't worry, you can make it up to me by coming to our first exhibition race."

"I feel like you're using this race to get me outside the office for your pleasure."

Watching the audience she had around her, I suggested walking over to her office and finishing this conversation.

"How about we go back to your office and negotiate the terms of you handling my account?"

"Mr. Pierce..."

"Jackson."

"I prefer Mr. Pierce. Besides, Dominique is handling the day-to-day business with your account. If there's something she can't handle, then she'll contact me, and we'll meet to discuss any outstanding questions."

Stepping closer to her, I could feel her breath hitch and her breasts swell as my chest pressed up closer. Noticing she was getting flustered with our closeness, I ran my palm against her soft jawline and cheek.

"Emery, the last thing you want to do with me is play games, baby."

"Emery, I thought that was you over here with Jackson," Dominique stated.

"Mr. Pierce," I informed.

"Excuse me." Dominique stepped closer to me as Emery stepped back.

"I'd like for you to call me Mr. Pierce."

"Ohhh... ummm sure, Jack... Mr. Pierce. Emery, can I speak with you for a minute?"

"Of course," Emery answered.

Buttoning up my coat, I allowed Dominique to pull Emery away from me.

"Emery, we'll finish this discussion another time," I told her, turning around and walking toward the elevator. I knew I'd need a replay of last night as I watched the sway of Emery's hips and ass in her knee-length skirt as she walked toward her office, plotting how to get her to dinner.

Chapter Six

Jackson

After leaving Emery, I needed to get some work done. Getting off the elevator on my office floor, I noticed my cousin Kimberly pop up out of her seat and follow me into my office.

"Jackson, you have two meetings back to..."

Opening the door, we both got the shock of our lives as my ex-girlfriend lay across my desk in nothing but her negligée and high heels.

"What the fuck, Jessica? Put your coat on!"

Kimberly shook her head and walked out of my office. I closed the door with a scowl on my face.

"I'm sorry, baby. Let me make it up to you." Jessica walked seductively over to me. We broke up a year ago after she cheated on me. She was around five feet seven with a mixture of hazelnut and toffee skin. Slender figure and large breasts, she used to be a model, but after we started dating, she became too comfortable with my money and quit working.

"Baby, I miss you." Jessica caressed my chest and

leaned up to kiss my lips. I turned my head to avoid her lips, and she kissed my right cheek.

"Why are you here, Jessica?"

"Is that any way to speak to the mother of your child?"

Closing my eyes in frustration, I grabbed her hands to move them away from me. I walked over to my desk and sat in my chair. I shook my head when she tried to come closer and pointed to the chair in front of my desk.

"Again, why are you here?

"Jackson, why can't we get back together? We both lost a child, and I'm seeing a therapist now. We could go into couples counseling to figure out how we can heal."

"I've moved on, and you moved on, or are you forgetting me catching you with your photographer buddy in your hotel room."

"That was a mistake, and I apologized to you about that. I was still hurting from losing our baby. You worked night and day to get over it. Twenty-four hours a day, while I stayed home grieving!"

"Jessica..."

"No, you don't get to dismiss me like that! We love each other!"

Kimberly rushed in after hearing Jessica yelling.

"What the hell's going on in here?" Kimberly asked, looking from Jessica to me.

"None of your business," Jessica remarked.

"Jessica, I suggest you take your stank attitude somewhere else. Because we both know you can't whoop my ass."

"Kim, I'm fine. Jessica is just leaving."

"No, we have to discuss this!" Jessica shouted.

"I'll call security," Kimberly replied and walked back out.

"You have to leave. I have another meeting. Nothing you say will cause me to give you another chance. I've moved on already."

She dropped her shoulders in defeat and bit her bottom lip as tears poured out of her eyes.

"Who is she?"

"You don't know her. Now if you'll excuse me."

She picked up her purse and keys off the floor right as security popped in behind Kimberly.

"Do we have a problem, Mr. Pierce?" the officer asked.

"This isn't over, Jackson. I'll meet you at your place tonight for dinner. Kimberly, I would say it was nice seeing you again, but we both know I'd be lying," Jessica sarcastically stated and walked out with her coat open, showing off her body in her negligee, bra, and panties.

"Whatever."

Watching Kimberly pour a glass of brandy for herself and one for me, I laughed in amusement at her lack of office etiquette.

"What?"

"You do realize you're at work, and I'm the boss."

Shrugging her shoulders, she took another shot of brandy and passed me a glass.

"You do realize I hate your ex-girlfriend, and the entire family wonders if we should commit you into a psychiatric ward for bringing her around us."

"I wouldn't fight you on that. But, honestly, at one point, Jessica was my world, and she didn't act this way. After she lost the baby, something changed, and she just became this money-hungry, celebrity-chasing star."

"Yeah, I've seen her on all the blogs with different guys. I suggest you get her tested before dipping back into that pool," Kimberly joked.

Waving her statement off, I gathered my notes and got ready for my meeting.

"Who is the first meeting with?"

"Brent sent over one of his contacts. A guy named Anthony Davis, a well-known designer in the business."

"Okay, send him in, and let's get going. I have a date tonight I can't miss."

"Ohhh! Who's the lucky girl?" Kimberly clapped her hands in excitement and sat on top of my desk.

"You must have forgotten Jessica was just lying on top of my desk in just a negligee."

"Ick! I have to get a tetanus shot now."

"Kim?"

"I'm serious. That girl's had more miles on her than our first NASCAR race at the start of your company. I'm surprised you haven't caught anything."

"I do worry about you."

"You know I only speak the truth. Besides, who keeps you laughing during those boring meetings and dinners?"

She opened the door to allow my first client to come inside.

"Mr. Davis. Welcome to Pierce Enterprises."

Chapter Seven

Emery

Listening to Dominique ramble on and on about Jackson and her dating made me nauseous.

"Dominique, I have a—"

"Seriously, Emery, you need to leave Jackson alone. I've already claimed him for myself."

Tired of her attitude, I rose out of my seat and walked up to her with my arms folded across my chest.

"Let me remind you, since you seem to forget. You work for me. My name is on that door as Executive VP. Neither one of us is dating Mr. Pierce because he's a client and if I find out you're making advances toward him—"

"Emery, I need your help!" Angela screamed as she burst through my door with Brent chasing right behind her.

"Angela, get your ass over here now!" Brent yelled angrily.

"No!" Angela shouted as she dodged his arms and ran behind me.

"Brent, what's going on?" I questioned.

Angela pulled me in tighter, nearly choking me to avoid Brent's reach.

"She just interrupted a critical meeting with some clients. Walking in like she runs things, demanding to have a client wear pant suits, shades, a wig, and stay twenty feet away from me at all times."

"Angela..." I exhaled in annoyance

"Well, she had no business coming onto you," Angela muttered softly.

"Who was the client?"

"Chanel Goldstein."

"Are you talking about the Goldsteins that own all of downtown and the shopping stores in Manhattan?"

"Yes... Emery, move out of the way."

Seeing Brent take off his belt, I knew it was time for me to go home.

"What are you doing?" Angela shrieked.

"What does it look like, sweetheart? You want to act like a brat, I'll treat you like one. If you ladies don't want to see your friend get a spanking, I suggest you leave now."

"Uhhh... Brent, you're in my office."

"And you're all in my building. So, leave before you see something you'll regret."

"I won't regret it. About time someone put her in her place," Dominique snidely remarked and sat to watch the show.

"Why did I come into work today?" I muttered.

Angela ran to the bathroom and locked herself inside. Brent rushed over and banged on the door.

"I'm leaving for the day, Brent. Whatever you do, don't have sex in my office please."

"Emery, don't leave me!" Angela yelled from the other side of the bathroom door.

"Sorry, Angie, next time you'll think twice before jumping in other folks' business," I answered as I led Dominique out, so Brent and Angela could finish their conversation.

"He could do so much better," Dominique stated.

"And who would you suggest he—"

My phone interrupted our conversation. I looked down to see Anthony's name across the screen. I debated on picking it up, but I knew he'd keep calling, I decided to answer and listen to his latest apology.

"Hello?" Anthony said on the other line.

"Yes, Anthony."

"Baby, I need to talk with you."

"First off, I'm not your baby. Secondly, we have nothing to discuss. The second your dick went into another woman's pussy, our relationship became null and void," I replied angrily.

Turning away from Dominique, I punched the button for the elevator.

"Anthony, call Teresa, or did she leave you already?"

"Arghhh... Emery, just let me make it right. Teresa means nothing to me," Anthony groaned through the phone in aggravation.

"Funny you say that when she's pregnant, wearing your ring, and living with you."

Hearing a beeping noise through my phone, I ended the conversation with Anthony.

"I have another call. Please delete my number. You've done enough damage to my heart to last a lifetime." Feeling a migraine coming on, I clicked over to answer the other end.

"Hello?"

"Dinner, my place tonight," Jackson seductively demanded.

"I thought we had an understanding, Mr. Pierce."

"I thought you knew to call me Mr. Pierce only in the bedroom."

Feeling weak in the knees from our first encounter, I reminded myself that getting involved with a client would lead down a destructive path.

"I already have plans. Besides, you're a client."

"Then you're fired."

"What!" I yelled out.

"Emery, what you fail to realize is that when I kissed your lips and tasted your sweet nectar, I was hooked, and nothing will keep me from having you again," Jackson responded.

Closing my eyes as the elevator doors opened, I tried to gather the strength to walk to my car.

"Are you wet, Ms. Stone?" Jackson asked.

Flushed and embarrassed at his question, I dropped my keys on the ground. As I bent over, I felt faint, and his voice sounded muted like it was under water. Dark spots appeared in my vision before I knew nothing at all.

"Hello? Emery! Emery!" Jackson shouted through the phone.

Chapter Eight

Jordan

Pulling up to the parking lot of my son's daycare center, I jumped out and headed inside to pick him up. I rushed through the doors and collided into a hard body, and two strong arms tried to steady me.

"Damn, you all right, Choc?"

"Huh?" I responded as I stared into light-brown eyes and deep dimples. I felt like I was having an orgasm from just looking at him. *That's not possible.*

Two fingers snapped in front of my face. I blinked out of my lust-filled trance.

"What did you call me?"

"Choc," he replied with a stunning smile.

"What does Choc mean?"

"Sorry, sweetness, but you're beautiful as milk chocolate. He glanced down at my hand and noticed I wasn't wearing a ring before continuing, "My favorite type of candy."

"Ohh... umm... well, thanks. But I need to..."

Tightening his hold on me, he pulled me in closer,

and I smelled his cologne. The same brand Devin used to wear, Tom Ford Musk 1991.

"Sorry, Choc, I can't let you go until I get your number. It must be fate that we met like this. I don't know about you, but I won't pass this chance up. Let me take you out," he suggested.

I shook my head no and pulled away from him.

"I'm sorry, Mr...."

"Damon Adams."

"Mr. Adams."

"Damon, and you are?"

"Jordan Davis."

"Nice to meet you, Choc."

Smirking at his comment, I shook my head and turned to look around to make sure the teachers hadn't dismissed the students yet.

"Jordan is my name, and Mr. Adams—"

"Call me Damon, beautiful."

"Fine, Damon... I don't date, and I'm here picking up my son."

"Small world. I'm picking up my daughter. What class is he in?"

"I'm not in the habit of giving out my private business to strangers. Check with some of the teachers around here. They may be right up your alley."

I turned and walked away, praying he couldn't smell my arousal from the throbbing heat between my legs. I needed a release and standing in his arms didn't help.

"How about lunch?" he called out.

"No."

"How about dinner?"

"No."

"How about ice cream?"

"No—"

"Yeah, Mommy, ice cream!" Devin Jr. screamed excitedly, running into my legs.

"Hi, Mrs. Davis. He couldn't wait to see you and show off the picture he drew," DJ's teacher Amy Lawrence stated.

I rolled my eyes at Damon's smug look at my son's outburst for ice cream, probably hoping to guilt me into complying.

"Baby, you have to eat first." I bent down to kiss DJ on the forehead. He pouted, crossed his arms, and stomped his feet.

"Mr. Adams, Tessa should be coming out of the classroom any minute now. I didn't know you two knew each other."

"We don't," we both answered.

"That's going to change real soon though," Damon answered, smiling at me and winking.

"Hi, Daddy." Tessa, Damon's daughter, came around the corner and raised her arms up toward him, so he could pick her up.

He leaned down, kissed her forehead, raised her up to his chest, and hugged her tight. "How was class, sweet pea?" Damon asked.

"Okay, how do you know DJ?" Tessa asked as she squirmed to get down. He placed her back down on the floor and watched as she walked over to DJ and me.

"This is your friend DJ that you talk about all the time?" Damon smirked and winked at me again as his daughter nodded her head at his question.

"Hi, Tessa, I'm DJ's mom. Nice to finally meet you."

She waved and smiled at me with her two front teeth

missing. She grabbed the crayons from DJ's hand and drew on her sheet of paper.

"Mommy, can we get ice cream please?"

"Yay, ice cream!" Tessa shouted in excitement.

"How about pizza and ice cream? Would you guys like that?" Damon encouraged both kids. Both children jumped up and down with excitement. "I guess that's three against one."

"You just bribed my son and your daughter into getting a date with me." Feeling a losing battle happening, I agreed to have dinner with Tessa and her father.

I pulled DJ's backpack off his shoulders and walked to the door. He opened it for the kids and me to walk out. We headed toward my car.

"Beautiful, I don't know what you're talking about. The kids need to eat, and I assume you need to eat as well."

Furious and annoyed at getting manipulated into dinner with the kids, I helped DJ into his car seat and buckled his seatbelt. Closing the door, I turned around, and Damon and I stared intensely into each other's eyes.

"Uggh, I'll follow you."

"Meet me at Roberto's over on 75th. They have the best pizza in town."

Walking around to the driver's side, Damon opened the door, and I dropped my purse inside and placed the key in the ignition. He closed the door and leaned into the window.

"I know how long it takes from here to Roberto's, Jordan. Don't try to skip out on me." He smiled, and they walked over to get in his car.

I placed my head down on the horn in frustration and

aggravation. Damon had already started with the little amount of time we'd known each other.

Bap! Bap!

"Ohh shit!"

Damon pulled alongside me, honking his car horn.

"Ahhh, Mommy, you said a bad word."

Rolling my eyes in annoyance, I started my car and pulled off behind Damon.

Chapter Nine

Emery

Scrolling through my phone while sitting in the hospital room and waiting for the doctor to discharge me, I came across my last text message exchange with Jackson.

Jackson: Dinner?

Jackson: Emery?

Jackson: You seriously want to play these games?

Seeing the doctor come into my room, I turned my phone off and waited to contact him back.

"Emery, you have to slow it down. Your blood pressure was through the roof. I highly recommend you take a vacation before you're permanently in the hospital," Doctor Langley said.

Agreeing to her orders was the only way she'd let me out of here. I replied, agreeing to take some time off, even though it would never happen, especially now that I had a massive deal with Pierce Enterprises happening.

"I will, Doctor. My family is having a reunion next month. I know Mom would love it if I took time off and relaxed."

"You're still in the early stages. You're already aware that flare-ups will happen if you're stressed. Lupus is manageable, Emery, but you need to take better care of yourself."

"I know."

"What about your family? Have they helped to keep things manageable in your life?"

So far, I had hidden my lupus diagnosis from my family and friends. Doctor Langley was pressing my buttons.

"I haven't talked with my family just yet. After I close this deal with a client, I'll fill everyone in on it. I promise."

Doctor Langley tapped her pen against her clipboard and furrowed her brow.

"Emery Stone, you can't do everything. I understand you believe you're superwoman, but honey, this is not curable. Manageable, yes; curable, no. I suggest you inform your family and seek therapy."

Feeling my phone vibrate, I took it out of my pocket and saw a message from my mom.

"I promise after this deal closes. Am I free to go?"

"Fine. Make sure you continue taking your medicine, and I'll see you in my office in two weeks."

Stepping down off the hospital bed, I picked up my purse and stepped into my shoes. Taking my discharge papers and signing out, I walked out of the cold hospital room and called for a cab.

* * *

Twenty minutes later, the cab pulled up to my grandmother's home. Noticing a lot of cars parked out front, I pulled out my mirror and checked my makeup and hair.

"Sugarplum, look at you." Grandfather Joe opened the door.

"Hi, Grandpa. It smells good in here." Pulling away from his hug, I looked around the room at some of my cousins, aunts, and uncles laughing and joking.

"Joe, who's at my door!" Grandmother yelled.

"Woman, stop yelling. It's my sugarplum. Come on in, sweet pea."

"Don't tell me what to do. I can yell if I want to."

"Momma, calm down. You just got out of the hospital."

Waving my mom off, my grandmother walked into the living room, wiping her hands on her apron.

"Now, don't you look like shit," Grandmother stated.

"Damn!" Stacy and Stephanie shouted at the same time.

"Grandma, really?" I replied.

"Baby, I call it as I see it. And sweetie, you look like the worst part of a Tyler Perry Madea movie."

Everyone burst out laughing, including myself.

"That woman is a mess," Grandfather stated.

Walking over to hug my grandmother, she cupped my chin and turned my head from left to right.

"What?"

"Uhmm... huh..."

"What?"

"We'll talk later. You hungry?"

"Yes, ma'am."

"All right, dinner is ready. Everybody, come on in the dining room."

Pulling my phone out, I texted Jackson back, apologizing for canceling on him.

Me: Sorry, family situation to handle.

Jackson: Rain check with dessert ;)

Biting my bottom lip in knowing the type of dessert he would be serving with his nine-inch, thick, and veiny cock.

"Who are you texting, little girl?"

"Huh?"

"If you can huh, you can hear. Who are you texting?"

"Grandma, did you make your famous mac and cheese?"

Washing my hands and drying them off, I walked back into the dining area, hugging and kissing my grandfather and my dad before taking the seat between them.

"You think you slick."

"Woman, leave Emery alone and fix my plate."

Rolling her eyes at her husband of forty years, she grabbed his plate like she'd been doing for the last forty years and put his dinner together. Finally, she leaned down and kissed his lips, and he patted her behind. She took off her apron, made her plate, sat next to him, and grabbed his hand.

Knowing the type of love they had and the obstacles they'd faced brought a smile to my face. She was the loudmouth, and he was the calm one of the two. Everyone believed she ran the house and marriage, but deep down, nothing moved in this family without Joe Anderson agreeing to it. My mom married my dad, and he was just like my grandfather. He let her think she ran things, when deep down, my mom wouldn't make a decision without talking with my dad first.

"Emery, did you see Brent after work today?"

Angela walked in and kissed my parents and grand-parents before taking a seat. Ever since her parents divorced when she was a little girl, she'd been a part of our family. Being raised by a single parent, many times her mom dropped her off at my house or grandparents' home while her mom worked two and three jobs.

"Don't you remember, Angela? I left as Brent was chasing you into the bathroom with a belt."

All talk and noise stopped. Realizing what I just said, I needed to clear the air before my dad and cousins went out looking for Brent. One thing about the men in my family, we may fight hard, but when it came to protecting the women, no doubt you'd come up missing.

"Damn, I remember those days when Joe used to chase me around. I pretended to be a bank robber, and you were the security guard. Remember, Joe? If you didn't have a bad knee now, we could've continued."

"I think I'm going to be sick," Mother whispered lowly.

"Hush, Elisabeth. How do you think you got here?"

"Through prayer!" Mother snapped back.

"You're right. I prayed your daddy wouldn't put that big thang in me..."

"Mom."

"Grandma!" we all shouted at the same time.

I picked up the glass of water and took a sip, since my appetite was gone now.

"I left a few minutes after you did, Emery. He had some business meeting to go to," Angela informed her.

Shrugging my shoulders, I picked up my phone to text Jackson back. I ignored everyone at the dinner table.

Me: My place or yours?

Jackson: Mine.

Me: Okay, give me twenty minutes.

Jackson: ...

"Who has you smiling?" Angela asked.

"None of your business," I replied.

Popping her lips, I took another sip of my water and winked back at her irritation. Standing up to leave, I walked around and kissed my grandparents, mother, and father.

"Make sure he straps up."

"Grandma. Who taught you that word?"

"Honey, how you think your mother got here?"

"What!" Elisabeth shrieked in aggravation.

Waving her daughter off, my grandmother hugged me and whispered in my ear, "Make sure you let him. I want to meet the man that has you glowing, and it ain't from pregnancy. Not yet anyway."

"Mother!" Elisabeth shouted.

"What, child? She's grown, we're grown. Hell, how you think she got here? I know he knocked you up before marriage. I still love my Emery, but I can't say I wasn't a little disappointed she came before marriage."

"Okay, time for me to go. Bye, everyone. Thanks for dinner, Grandma," I stated.

I pulled out my phone and called for a Lyft ride. Thirty minutes later, we pulled up in front of Jackson's ten-thousand-square-foot home.

"Wow."

Getting out of the car and walking to the door, it opened, and an older gentleman wearing a suit and tie greeted me.

"Hello, Ms. Stone."

"Hello, just Emery please."

"Of course. I'm Ronald Jacobson, Mr. Pierce's house manager. He's in the foyer room waiting for you."

Walking into his home, I saw large, high ceilings, open floor space with a widening staircase at the entrance, and beautiful African art pieces hanging on both sides of the wall.

"Here you are, Mr. Jackson."

Jackson stood with his back to us, wearing a white tee shirt, grey sweatpants, and Nike slides—something completely different from his usual suit and tie.

"Hi."

Turning and staring into my eyes lustfully, I could feel the throbbing ache between my thighs.

"Have you eaten?"

Moving closer into the foyer, I tried holding eye contact, but his intense gaze had me rethinking this entire meeting.

"I ate a little."

"Why did you hang up on me earlier?"

"I... I..." I stuttered, not wanting to tell him the truth.

"Emery, you'll learn that I don't have much patience for liars. I spoke with Brent, and he told me you left your office around eleven this morning, and you're just returning my text at eight pm. So again, I ask why you hung up on me earlier?"

Roaming my eyes around the room, I tried to avoid answering his question. I made a rash decision to distract him. I walked over to him to brush my fingers against his lips. Leaning up, I buried my face in his neck. He wrapped his arms around my waist as his breathing increased.

Picking me up, I wrapped my legs around his waist, and we fell onto the couch with him lying on top of me.

We fought for dominance of the kiss; his tongue won in the end.

"Mmmhmm," I whimpered.

Stopping our kiss, he leaned up away from my face and stared into my eyes.

"After tonight, I don't want to hear anything about this fake dating rule with clients. Do we understand each other?"

Nodding in agreement, I leaned up and captured his lips. He moaned into my mouth.

"Ughhh," Jackson groaned.

He bent over and buried his face into my neck and kissed behind my ear, locking my legs around his waist to pull him in closer. I ran my hand up and down his arm and attempted to give him pain and pleasure as he gave me the first night we had sex. I bit along his cheek and chin.

"Fuck me," I moaned against his lips.

"Are you mine, Emery?"

"Yesssss," I shuddered in his arms, as he moved down my chest, kissing and biting. Twisting my nipples through my shirt, he ran a hand up and down to my skirt and spread my legs wider. Pulling my panties off, he started at my ankles and worked his way down to my second lips and sniffed, then licked.

"Ohhh my God!"

"Fuck, you taste good, baby."

"Jackson, please."

Leaning up on my elbows, I watched as he made love to my pussy. Feeling the intensity, I moved my hips in time with his teasing. He used his two index fingers to play with my clit.

"Aahhh..." My eyes closed at the feel of his fingers playing in my dripping and soaking wetness.

"I need to be inside you, baby."

"Shittt... Jackson."

Toying with his thick member out of his sweatpants, I watched as he placed a condom on and ran his penis up and down my slick folds.

"Emery, look at me."

I shook my head, not wanting to look him in the eye. I knew we were building a real connection. I promised myself after Anthony, I would never give my heart to another man again.

"Baby, look at me... shit." Jackson hissed as he slowly pushed into my pelvis.

"Aahh... fuck... wait."

I tried shoving him away. Forgetting how thick he was. I must have been drunk not to remember his girth.

"You want me to pull out?"

His strokes were long and penetrating. Pushing my legs back further to get more room, I felt him in my chest.

"God... ohhh... God!" I moaned loudly.

I cried out, hoping none of his staff heard me. Pulling him back into me for a kiss, he sped his strokes up, and I met his pace as my first orgasm came over me.

"Yessss... Baby!" He grabbed my breasts as he pulled out and smacked my left thigh to turn around. Feeling weak from the work he put me through, I slowly rolled over and leaned over the couch, gripping the cushion and spreading my legs further apart.

Spanking my left and right butt cheeks, he bent down and ran his tongue up and down my wet folds. Stiffening his tongue, he darted in and out fast, then slow. Juices flowed on his tongue and down my leg.

"You taste like peaches, baby," Jackson moaned behind me.

"Ughhh... Fuck." My lips pursed and vision blurred at the sensation. I took in a sharp breath, feeling his tongue. He penetrated my lower lips with his finger as his tongue darted into my backside. I felt an otherworldly sensation and jumped away from the double pleasure.

"Jackson, I've never done backdoor play."

"Baby, one thing you'll learn about me is that I'm a grown man, and we're both consenting adults. We can take it slow for now."

Pulling my back to his chest, he leaned me over the couch further to raise my ass higher in the air. Slapping his dick against my swollen clit, I pushed onto him and stopped, feeling my orgasm creep up slowly.

"Fuckkk... Sweetness, you feel so good," Jackson growled as his pace picked up.

Feeling my orgasm building, I glanced down and watched as his balls smacked up against my thighs and heard his moans in my ear.

"Aahhh, Jackson."

"You're mine, Emery. Do you hear me?"

He yanked my hair, and my head snapped back as his strokes grew more in-depth and faster. "I can't... hear you, sweetness."

My lips parted at the sensation brewing between my legs.

"Yes... baby... Yes!" I screamed.

We both came at the same time, and he fell on top of me as we both tried to calm our heavy breathing. Kissing the side of my face, I turned to meet his lips as we both smiled at the mess we made.

"Are you hungry?" Jackson asked as he slowly eased out of me and held my skirt up, so I could get dressed.

"Yeah, and I think both my legs are broken."

Pulling the condom off and grabbing his sweatpants, I followed him to the bathroom to freshen up.

"Where's the rest of your staff?"

"I gave everyone the night off. Ronald stays at the mansion. Did you think I'd fuck you with a house full of people?"

"No, just thought it was strange with all the moaning and screaming you were doing that no one came to your rescue."

"Sweetness, I'll gladly let you torture me any day if it's like that with your ass in the air."

Grabbing the wet towel out of his hand, I freshened up and brushed my teeth with the extra toothbrush laid out.

"You just knew I would sleep with you again, or another woman is coming over."

"What are you talking about?"

Narrowing my eyes at him, I pointed at the toothbrush and clothes resting on the counter.

"I should spank you again for thinking I would bring you to my home after another woman. If you must know, Emery Stone, you're the first woman to ever come to my house. All other sleepovers happened at a hotel," Jackson responded.

"Seriously?"

"Yep, now let's jump in the shower and go eat. I'm ready for round three and four. I feel insulted by that remark."

"Aahh, poor baby, I hurt your feelings. What can I do to make you feel better?"

Dropping his sweatpants and taking off his shirt, we both looked down at the hardening of his dick again.

"I can think of a few things," Jackson responded.

Smiling at his suggestion, I took my skirt and shirt off, leaving on my bra and panties. Dropping to my knees, I grabbed ahold of his dick and squeezed it gently.

"Yes, Mr. Pierce."

* * *

Three hours and two orgasms later, we ended up at *Gem's,* a new restaurant that just opened about eight months ago. Jackson held my chair out, and I sat and picked up the menu. He leaned down and kissed me on the forehead, making me blush.

"You better stop before we end up on top of this table, going for round five, or is it six. I can't remember," I joked.

"That wouldn't be such a bad idea, sweetness. Especially since we came at the right time. There's barely anyone in here."

Jackson was a man who made you want to wake up every morning early and make breakfast and serve it naked. Laughing off my thoughts, I knew a real commitment could never happen. Anthony turned my heart so bitter, men only helped for one thing, and that was having an orgasm.

"Emery! Emery! Are you all right? I was calling your name."

"I'm sorry, I was lost in thought. What did you ask?"

"Do you have any idea what you'd like for dinner? I heard the pasta and steak are delicious."

"I'll have whatever you're getting and a glass of wine."

The waitress came over, and we passed our menus

over after placing our order. Jackson picked my hand up and kissed both sides, making me melt from his warmth. Gathering my thoughts, I let my hand fall away, hoping not to get caught up in his whirlwind romance.

"You know this isn't a date, right?"

"Why do you do that?" Jackson asked.

"Jackson, we had a one-night stand and then a repeat. You know what this is and how it plays out. The media would have a field day if they suspected you're dating again. We're from two different worlds."

"I can handle the media and whoever else chimes in on what I do in my private life."

Control was something I couldn't give up, and I could see we would butt heads in and out of the bedroom.

"Can we please just finish dinner first and let everything else go until tomorrow?"

"You got it," Jackson replied and took a sip from his glass of wine right when our dinner came to the table.

Chapter Ten

Jordan

Placing a sleepy DJ in his car seat after our dinner with Tessa and Damon, I covered him up with his blanket before shutting the passenger-side door. "Thanks for dinner. I think the kids enjoyed themselves."

Turning to leave, Damon gently grabbed my elbow and pulled me in until we were chest to chest. I felt my breathing picking up. He leaned down to kiss me, and I turned my head before our lips could touch.

"I can't," I whispered and stepped out of his grip, before rushing over to the driver's side. Looking in my rearview mirror, I saw him standing at the curb with his hands in his pockets with a defeated look on his face.

We arrived home, and I picked up DJ out of his car seat and walked into the condo we shared with Angela.

Hearing music blasting, I took DJ into his room and placed him down on the bed to take his shoes and jacket off, reminding myself to give him a bath in the morning. Placing the covers over him and turning his night light on,

I closed the door and walked into the kitchen to grab a bottle of water.

"Hey, you're home late," Angela stated, walking into the kitchen with rollers in her hair and a facial mask, wearing Brent's housecoat.

"Yep, late dinner. How was your day?" I asked, closing the fridge door and opening the bottle to take a sip.

"Fine, just handling business at the salon, then dinner with the family. Have you spoken with Emery today? I heard Anthony's still calling and harassing her."

"He's crazy, and I told him multiple times to leave that girl alone. Emery's moved on from him. He decided to step out on her and expects her to forgive and forget. Especially with nasty Teresa."

"Angela, baby, come back to bed." Brent walked out in his pajama bottoms and no shirt, rubbing the crust out of his eyes.

"I see someone's forgiven his girlfriend. What did she do this time, Brent?"

"Shut up, Jordan. If you must know, I'm only his girl-friend inside these walls. Outside of here, we're just close friends."

"Angela, you don't want to get slapped," Brent chas-tised playfully and snuggled up against her body.

"Boy, please, you know who runs this." She pointed between herself and Brent.

I held in my laughter at the back-and-forth banter they continued to have after dating on and off since college.

"Since you're not my girl, I guess I can call up one of my other friends to help relieve stress," Brent joked and walked over to pick up the telephone in the kitchen.

"Are you talking about that girl Emery and I met when we ran into you at lunch last month?" Playing along with his joke, I waited to see what Angela would do as Brent started to dial a number.

Angela poked out her lip, moved her weight from one foot to the other, and crossed her arms.

"What tramp did you have lunch with last month, Brent?"

"None of your business. I only answer to my girlfriend."

"Okay, Okay... damn it," Angela whined in protest.

"Okay, what?" Brent asked.

"We're together," Angela mumbled in a whisper.

"Sorry, what was that?" I asked loudly.

"Stay out of this, J. This is between the big-headed idiot and me over here." Angela popped her lips and grabbed the phone from Brent.

"Dial the slut's number, and I dare you to say anything. I'm ending whatever side chick situation you had going on."

Brent dialed the number and placed it on speaker. He winked at me and placed his finger over his mouth, signaling for me to be quiet.

"Hello?" a woman groggily replied.

"Hello, yeah, I'm calling to tell you to stay away from Brent Townsend. He's got a girlfriend, and you are no longer needed. Excuse me... I'm sorry, Miss Townsend," Angela muttered lowly.

Brent and I both broke out in laughter at her mistaking Brent's mother for a girl he was dating. She hung up the phone, turned toward us, and flipped us off before she walked off toward the bedroom. Brent followed her, trying to get her to soften up.

"Baby, you have to admit that was funny, and you deserved it," Brent told her.

"Are you done? I'd like to get some sleep now since you've kept me up all night playing little boy games. Do you see why I don't do relationships?" Angela muttered to herself.

Brent stopped laughing and cleared his throat. Stepping closer to her, he towered over her five-five frame. Wrapping his arms around her waist, he tightened his hold on her and pushed her gently up against the wall.

"Angela, I love you, and I've dealt with your shit for over five years. But let's get one thing straight... I won't continue to let you disrespect me, and you know this. I suggest you change your attitude and fast. I let you and other people think you're running this between us, but we both know the truth. Now kiss me, take your clothes off, and get into position," Brent demanded sternly.

"Yes, Daddy," Angela replied sexily.

"And tomorrow, you're moving in with me. Jordan needs her space, and I need you with me at night in my bed," Brent informed.

"Hell no..." Angela responded loudly.

"What did I just say?"

"But—"

"Either you're moving forward with me, or we're just friends and no benefits. I'm too old to be playing games with you, Angela."

"Fine, I want a walk-in closet," Angela told him while stomping into her bedroom.

"Whatever you say, baby," Brent replied and smacked her on the butt.

"You two are a mess," I mumbled to myself.

"I swear if I didn't love her, this would have ended a

long time ago. She's stubborn, loud, sassy, likes to lead anything we have planned."

"So why are you with her again?"

He shrugged his shoulders and ran a hand down his face in frustration.

"That's my baby; she can be all those things. But let somebody else call her crazy, and I'd knock them out."

"Well, it's nice to see you've finally tamed the beast."

"Hey, watch it now. She's your best friend."

Waving off Brent's comment, I grabbed a glass and poured some wine as Brent came closer into the kitchen.

"I see the bottle is out. I know I'm not Angela or Emery, but I've been known to give some great advice. Tell your play brother what's up."

"Nothing, you wouldn't understand. Besides, Angela's waiting on you in the room."

Hearing the music turning up let us both know she was getting impatient.

"She'll wait, so tell me what has you drinking at this time of night. I know after Devin's death, you've been raising DJ alone, and your brother's shit has gotten everyone pissed at him. So, the stress has to be building up."

Sighing in relief that I could talk to someone and not feel judged had me wanting to open up more than ever.

"I met someone today."

"Okay, and that's a bad thing why?"

"Because I feel guilty for dating. What if DJ hates me for bringing someone around who's not his father."

"Whoa... now, how many dates have you gone on with him?"

Gulping another glass down, Brent took the bottle out of my hands and screwed the top back on.

"I can handle my liquor, Brent. I'm not Angela." I walked off and sat on the couch, pulling off my shoes. He followed behind me and plopped down next to me.

"Thank God there's only one Angela in the world. Many times, I've questioned if she was dropped on her head when she was born."

We both busted out in laughter at his comment, and he nudged me in the shoulder to continue talking.

"He's a parent at the school, and we met today. Well, we bumped into each other, and he wouldn't let me leave without giving him my number or having dinner. Somehow his daughter and DJ are friends in the same class, and they heard ice cream, so of course, he wouldn't deny his daughter anything she wants."

Hearing Brent laughing under his breath, I smacked him upside the head for taking my dilemma as a joke.

"That's not funny, Brent."

"I'm sorry, J, but it's the oldest trick in the book. You have to admit the guy has skills."

"Whatever."

Shaking his head at me, I stood and grabbed my shoes before walking toward my bedroom.

"Okay, Okay... I'm done messing with you. It was one date. Give it some time before you cut off all men. Besides, your kids are friends, so don't go messing up the little man's friendship."

Nodding in agreement, we both hugged and went in the opposite direction of our bedrooms.

"Thanks, Brent."

"Anytime, J. Remember, I'm here for you and DJ. That's my nephew, and you're my sister. Even though it's not by blood, you're family to me. Get some rest, and I'll drive DJ to school tomorrow."

"You don't have to do that."

"You and your girls need some time alone. I can already tell Angela's going to argue about me bossing on her. So, I'll make arrangements for you guys to get some spa time at that local salon she was talking about."

"Oh... the one that opened next door to her salon. ZeniibyInez?"

"Yeah, it's a locally owned business by a black woman, Inez Laval. So, we have to support our people. She even hosts a podcast show called Moscato something."

"I know what you're talking about. Moscato and Tea. I listen to it whenever I'm working out or driving to work."

Leaving a kiss on his cheek, I walked over to DJ's bedroom to make sure he was still asleep. Opening and closing his door, I walked back into my room, tossed my shoes by the closet, and checked my phone for any messages.

Seeing a new message from an unknown number, I opened it up and smirked in amusement.

555-486-6907: You know you owe me.

Me: Tony, stop playing on my phone.

555-486-6907- Who the fuck is Tony? This is Damon.

Falling back on the bed in laughter, I continued my banter.

Me: Whoops, sorry, my bad. How did you get my number?

I saved him in my phone under "Jackass" and waited for his response.

Jackass: Baby, did you forget at the school today, I took your phone and saved my number.

Me: Someone's a little ahead of themselves with using words of endearment.

Jackass: Jordan, you might as well let every guy know you're my wife. So, cut off all those little boys you've been dating now. Daddy's home.

Me: Blocked

Turning the light on in my room, I put my phone on to charge. I grabbed my nightclothes and headed to the bathroom to shower and get some sleep for tomorrow.

Chapter Eleven

Emery

Listening to Angela on the phone talking with Brent and watching Jordan text away on her phone, this so-called girl spa day was turning into a one-woman show.

"We're here, ladies."

"I'll call you back because I said so," Angela snapped into the phone.

"This is gorgeous. I can't wait to get pampered. She does facials and waxing." Jordan took the brochure off the counter as we stood in the lobby, signing in.

"You're pissing me off, Brent. I see no ring on my finger—" Angela rolled her eyes in frustration and walked back out the door.

Jordan and I turned around and saw her walking over to Brent's car in the parking lot. She ended the call, and he stepped out of the car, pulled her into his arms, and kissed her cheek.

"Those two will either end up married with ten kids or dead."

"Jordan, you have such a morbid sense of humor.

Now, who are you texting back and forth? You've been on your phone for the last thirty minutes ever since we left breakfast," I asked, being nosy.

She smiled and turned her phone off as a woman walked up to us, laughing with a glass of champagne in her hands.

"Welcome to ZeniibyInez, I'm Inez."

"Hi Inez, you have a beautiful spa. I'm Emery, and this is Jordan."

"Thanks, ladies. You're more than welcome to grab a glass of Moscato, and you can follow me back to the room."

"I love Moscato. Any chance you have anything stronger? My head hurts." Angela walked up behind us.

"Angela, it's ten in the morning."

"It's Happy Hour somewhere," Inez and Angela said at the same time and burst into laughter and slapping high five.

"I can see you two are going to be trouble," Jordan stated.

"Don't mind them. I'm ready for the facial, then waxing. I have a date tonight."

"I thought Brent said he had to work late tonight?" Jordan questioned.

"He does," Angela told her.

Jordan, Emery, and Inez all looked at Angela in shock. Jordan waved her off and stepped out of the room to go next door.

"You're determined to run that man away. Don't come crying to us when he leaves you for good this time."

"I'm not worried about Brent leaving me. He knows what it is with us. I never hid that I don't want to be tied down."

"Okay." Jordan walked out and left Angela with Inez as she headed to another waxing room.

* * *

Forty minutes later, we were sitting in the café area in our fluffy white robes, eating lunch and sipping on mimosas as other ladies chatted and ate. While looking around the spa with its high ceilings, cream-colored walls with gold trimmings, and an indoor pool, the waiter approached and placed our baked salmon and rice meal with fruit on the side down. We enjoyed the low music, playing Mariah Carey.

"We're best friends, so this is coming from love. Don't take offense."

"Okay." Angela placed her drink down as Jordan turned in her seat and put her hands in her lap.

"You're fucking up, and I need you to grow up before he leaves you."

"Excuse me?"

"Emery, please tell her how dumb she's acting."

Angela rolled her eyes at Jordan in annoyance and picked up her fork to eat her food.

"She's right, Angela; you need to stop playing games with Brent. The man's been running behind you for years."

"That's funny coming from you Emery. Have you taken any calls from Anthony?" Angela questioned.

Jordan's eyes widened in shock, and Angela smirked at me like she caught me red handed. Leaning onto the table, so no one heard me, "I have, and they ended with me blocking him after I told him we're through. So, before you try to come for me like I'm the enemy, you should look in your closet."

"What about that Jackson guy we met at the restaurant?"

"Nothing, we've had dinner a few times and slept together. I'm not in the right headspace to date someone exclusively. Work takes up a lot of my time."

"Did he ask you to marry him?"

"What? No."

"Then date the man. Somebody needs to clean out that cobweb between your thighs," Angela joked and picked up a piece of fruit off my plate. I smacked her hand as she dropped it and stuck her tongue out at me.

"You are so childish, Angela. I wonder how Brent puts up with you."

"Easy, the wetness between my thighs has him under control," Angela wiped her mouth with her napkin and took another sip of her drink.

"Anyway, what have you been up to, Jordan?" Giving my undivided attention to her, I could tell something was bothering her.

"Just missing Devin and raising DJ; that boy is growing so fast. I wish his father could be here."

"I heard someone's trying to make his presence known."

"Who?" I asked, shocked by her statement.

"Nobody." Jordan waved Angela's little comment off.

"Let me determine that, so who's this guy?"

"Angela, you have such a big mouth. Nothing to tell. He's a parent at DJ's school that I bumped into by accident."

"And that leads to a family dinner with the kids."

"Focus on your relationship please, and let her tell the

rest of the story," I told Angela before turning back to Jordan.

"His name's Damon Adams, and he has one daughter. She's beautiful, and my dumb ass hasn't even asked if he's still seeing her mother. We've been texting back and forth since yesterday."

"Sounds like you like him. Just give it time and see where it goes. Besides, Angela is right about one thing. We both get a chance to get the cobwebs cleaned out."

I smiled, and we all burst out in laughter. After we calmed down, Angela put her hand on Jordan's arm.

"I'm sorry. You still love me?"

"Yes, do I like you right now? Uhh, nope. But you can buy drinks to make up for all the drama." Jordan smiled at Angela. We finished our lunch, changed, and left, going our separate ways.

I pulled up to my apartment and saw Anthony sitting on my porch. Blowing out a breath in aggravation, I grabbed my groceries and purse and locked my door. He met halfway and took the bags out of my hands as I shook my head in disbelief at his arrogance to come to my place. Putting my purse and jacket down on the table, I followed him into the kitchen and stood at my door with my hands crossed against my chest. I waited for him to finish with his little game of being helpful before addressing him.

"I made a mistake."

"It's too late, Anthony." Turning and walking to my bedroom, I went to change clothes. He followed and grabbed me by the arm. I jerked away, and he raised both hands in surrender.

"Sorry. Listen, Emery, can we talk, please? I know this situation is messed up. But we love each other, and we can get through this if you give me a chance." Turning away from him, I continued toward my bedroom and shut the door. As I took my shirt off, he opened my bedroom door, and I rushed into the closet, surprised by him following me.

"GET OUT!"

"I've seen you naked before, baby," Tilting his head to the left, a small smirk came across his face as he sat on my bed.

Rolling my eyes, I continued changing my clothes. Hearing my phone ring, I walked out of my closet and saw Anthony answering my phone.

"Who is that?"

"You're calling my woman—"

I snatched away my phone before whoever was calling could hang up. "Hello?"

"Who's that answering your phone, sweetness?" Hearing Jackson calmly speaking into the phone gave me chills, wondering if his bite was worse than his bark.

I smacked Anthony's hand away and walked toward the window. "No one. Are you at the office?"

"Don't dismiss my question. I suggest you answer me before I come to where you are."

"Can I call you back?"

"No."

"Jack—"

"Who the fuck is Jack?" Anthony demanded.

"Please, Jackson... I'll call you right back."

"I'm giving you three minutes to get rid of your company for good before I do it for you."

"Fine."

"Emery, don't make me show my ass. I told you, sweetness, you are mine. Don't let the suit fool you; my reach is wide. Do you understand me?"

Feeling the lump in my throat, I closed my eyes and nodded in understanding as if he could see me. I hung up and ran my hands down my face.

"Emery, we can make this work." Anthony pulled me into a hug and kissed my forehead, then my cheek and lips. Falling deeper into his arms, I raised mine around his neck and returned his kiss. I pulled away abruptly when I realized I was with Anthony and not Jackson.

"I can't do this with you. Anthony, you repeatedly cheated with my best friend and got her pregnant. YOU BROKE US!"

"Babe, please... I'm sorry. We can get past this. Just give me a chance. I promise."

Pacing in front of my couch and watching him walk closer to me, I pushed him away and sat in the chair, taking deep breaths to gather my thoughts.

"I don't think—"

"Emery, don't. You know me; we're meant to be together. Yes, I made a mistake. At the time, you were working so much, and I was missing you and hearing what you were doing at work and around all those guys."

"Wait, what does me being around guys and working have to do with you cheating on me?"

"Teresa said you—"

"Before you finish that statement, I want you to think about what comes out of your mouth. Because if you're about to say that Teresa told you I was cheating with guys at my job, then you automatically believed her."

"What was I supposed to do, Emery?" Anthony knocked all the papers on my table to the floor.

"You were supposed to come to ME." Standing to get into his face, I pointed my finger and furrowed my right brow.

"She was there for me."

"And I was your girlfriend." Feeling tears in my eyes, I wiped them with my shirt and shook my head in disappointment. Swearing to myself to never cry over him again. Feeling my blood pressure rising, I knew I needed to calm down before I passed out, and Anthony found out about my secret. Hearing knocking at my door, I walked over and opened it, shocked by the person standing on the other side.

"You've got to be shitting me. Why are you here, Teresa?" I watched as she rubbed her pregnant belly in my face. Thinking it would make me jealous.

"I came to take my fiancé home. Seeing as how you keep calling and begging him to get back together." Teresa pushed me aside and walked into my apartment.

"Teresa, go home. I told you already, Emery and I are working on our relationship."

"WHAT!" Teresa and I shouted at the same time.

Watching her walk up to him and smack him across the face, I wanted so bad to slap her like that. Seeing her pregnant, I needed to keep my cool and get them both out of my apartment.

"Keep your hands to yourself, T."

"I'm here because we have a doctor's appointment. If you'd stop running behind Emery and focus on our baby and engagement, you'd see she's not good for you." Teresa plopped down on my couch and crossed her legs, shooting an evil glare at me.

"You and I both know that's not my baby. You've been sleeping with every guy at your job." Anthony went to help her up from the couch, and she smacked his hand away.

"So, you cheated on me with her, and she cheated on

you with someone else, and she's possibly not carrying your baby?" I asked, hoping to get final closure on this situation between the three of us.

Glaring at me and positioning herself toward Anthony, she raised off the couch and walked toward him.

"This is your baby. Stop telling that lie."

"I don't know that for sure. Until you have the baby, I'm single and working on my relationship with Emery."

"Um, I think not. Anthony, you need to leave and take Teresa with you. I'm so over this situation. I couldn't care less what you two do. I have plans tonight, and you're both holding me up."

"I'm not going anywhere until my fiancé leaves," Teresa stated and walked in front of me, crossing her arms and poking her lips out.

I reached for my ringing phone and answered it as they continued to argue.

"Are you alone?"

Feeling butterflies in my stomach, I walked over to the window and looked outside. Seeing a car parked down the street, I closed the drapes and walked to my door to get rid of Anthony and Teresa before Jackson came upstairs.

"No, Mr. Pierce."

"Emery..." Hearing the strain in his voice made me think back to the other night with him between my thighs and the push and pull of our bodies against each other.

"Yes... Mr. Pierce?"

"Are you determined to make me angry, sweetness?"

"There's a lot of things I'm determined to get from you, Mr. Pierce. Angry isn't one of them. Are you outside my apartment?"

"If I said yes, will you escort your guests out before I come up there and throw them out?"

"I'd rather not have the police at my door over you and Anthony fighting."

"Baby, one thing you won't have to worry about is calling the police."

"Give me one second, Jackson."

"Emery, who the hell is Jackson?" Anthony stepped right into my face with flaring nostrils and his chest heaving up and down.

"Ohh... she's stepping her game up. I knew you were a gold digger. Jackson's a billionaire owner of a race car franchise. She just got the account from Brent."

"Are you sleeping with him? Baby, we can work this out. I forgive you, okay? We both made mistakes, but I know we can make this work."

"I need you two to leave and stay away from me. Teresa, if you see me at work, go the opposite way." Pushing them both out the door, I slammed it shut and locked it.

"Sorry about that. I didn't invite Anthony over if you were thinking that."

"I know. But you need to remind your ex I don't play about what belongs to me."

"I don't recall saying I was your woman."

Hearing his laugh on the other end of the line, some of the stress I was feeling left as I lay back on the couch, pulling my hair out of the bun on top of my head.

"What are you wearing?"

"I'm not having phone sex with you, Jackson."

"I just asked what you are wearing and if I wanted phone sex, you'd give it to me."

"How do you know that?"

"Because you'd do anything to please me, and I'd do the same for you."

"I... I..." I stuttered out.

"Listen. How about we do lunch tomorrow after our meeting? I know a place by my office that would give us privacy."

"Why would we need privacy? Besides, I won't be at the meeting long because of back-to-back meetings. Dominique is leading it. I'll be there for backup."

"You're going to deny me."

"Yes. Unlike you, Mr. Pierce, I must work for a living. I don't own a billion-dollar company."

"In due time, sweetness. I'll let you get some work done. Oh, and Emery, I suggest you keep your ex out of your face before something happens."

"Jackson, nothing is going on between us. He's getting married, and I'm a grown woman. I can date whoever I want."

Walking to the kitchen to pull out a steak and potato for dinner tonight, I listened as something shuffled on the other end of the phone.

"I'll see you tomorrow, sweetness. Wear something sexy."

Smiling at his suggestion, I started to reply but instead, I hung up and continued making dinner. After eating and cleaning up the kitchen, I grabbed an outfit for tomorrow and set my alarm.

Chapter Twelve

Emery

Waking up with a hard-on from dreaming about Emery and our last conversation, I needed to make sure her ex wasn't sniffing around her again. From the first moment I saw her in the restaurant, wearing her hair up in a tight bun, with that beautiful smile, I knew I'd have her for myself. This thing between us always made me want to keep her with me. She was my peace on a crazy day.

I could see myself marrying and having kids with her someday. The media already had it out for me—playboy billionaire dating models and actresses. What they didn't know was most of the women they saw with me half the time, I didn't sleep with. It was mostly for appearance. At the end of the day, I was running a business, and if being seen in public with high-profile women brought more attention and advertisers to our company, then I needed to keep it up until Emery came around to the idea of us being together.

Rolling over to turn off my alarm and check my phone

for messages, I rose out of bed and pushed my erection down.

"Damn, I need to cut this meeting early."

Hearing my phone go off, I saw Brent texting a reminder about our three-on-three games this weekend. Replying that I was down for the time, I sent another text to Emery.

Me: Morning, beautiful.

Sweetness: Morning, Mr. Pierce.

Smirking at her using Mr. Piece again. I egged her on to see how far she'd go with this.

Me: Send me a photo of you naked sweetness

Sweetness: Yes, sir.

A picture came through of her lying on the bed, wearing nothing but heels and high-waisted stockings.

"Shit."

Me: Sweetness, be prepared for me to rip those stockings and clothes off you when I see you today. Oh, and you're coming home with me today.

Sweetness: Yes, sir. ;)

Saving the photo and shutting my phone off, I gathered my clothes for the day and headed to the shower. Two hours later, I walked into Brent's office.

"What's up, man?" Brent stepped from behind his desk and shook hands.

"Nothing much. You ready for this meeting today?" Brent sat back down and clicked on his intercom.

"Lisa, can you send in a cup of coffee for Jackson?"

"Is Emery here?"

"Why? Please don't tell me you're trying to ask her out."

"Actually, that's—"

Lisa walked in with a cup of coffee, cream, and sugar

for me. Placing it on the counter, I thanked her, and she walked back out.

"Listen, Jackson, Emery's like a little sister to me. We both know how you are with women. You get bored quickly and move on to the next available—"

"Don't even finish that sentence, man. You know as well as I do that she's special, and I don't need your permission."

"You're right, but if you hurt her, I will kick your ass. We're boys, but Emery, Jordan, and Angela mean the world to me."

"I get that, and before I ever come close to hurting her, I'd leave her alone first. So, can we get this meeting started? I have plans for Ms. Stone, and they don't involve being stuck in a meeting all day."

"Fine, let me check to see if Dominique's set the conference room up. Did you check out the preliminary ads she sent over?"

"I did, and they looked pretty good. We need to finalize some things, and then we can go ahead with the posters and billboards."

Brent picked some files up off his desk, turned the computer off, placed his jacket back on, and led us out of his office.

"Great, then let's get to the conference room."

Brent passed his secretary the files.

"Lisa, can you let Angela know I'm going to be running late for lunch." Brent grabbed a mint off Lisa's desk, popped it in his mouth, and walked with me to the larger conference room.

Pulling the door open, we noticed some of my team and Brent's already sitting and ready for the meeting. Glancing to the far end of the table, Emery was leaning over some guy in a suit with a frown on her face. Feeling the possessiveness come over me, I start to walk up on the conversation when Brent grabbed my elbow and motioned over to two gentlemen standing with my company logo shirts on.

"Jackson, I want you to meet Cody and Danny. They're handling the merchandising department and started with a few mock-up shirts for you to test out." Brent gestured for them to pass around the sample materials to the entire room.

"These look great, Brent. Did you use the material from a local factory?" I asked, looking over Cody's shoulder at Emery and Dominique talking in the corner. She must have felt my presence because she looked over at me and smiled. I smiled back and brought my attention back to Cody.

"Did you hear me?"

"I'm sorry, what?" I placed the shirt down on the table and picked up the file folder with the presentation paperwork.

"If you weren't so distracted by Emery, you would have heard me say we used a local business to create the shirts, and they're giving us a deal if you want to go with them for everything from shorts, hats, and socks to calendars and bookmarks." Brent chuckled, and I waved him off and walked around to sit next to Emery.

"All right, ladies, let's get this meeting started so Mr. Pierce can get back to his busy day," Brent joked and sat across from me as I glared at his remarks with narrowing eyes.

"Dominique, we're ready."

"Thanks, Brent. Mr. Pierce, again it's a pleasure to work on this project for you. I'm a huge fan of your work."

Out of the corner of my eye, I saw Emery rolling her eyes at Dominique kissing up to me. What she didn't get was that I only had eyes for one woman, and that was her.

"Thanks, Dominique. I appreciate the support. But you should thank your boss. Brent strong-armed me into doing business with him, and he picked you and Emery. I guess your work speaks for itself." She nodded and started the presentation. Two hours later, everyone shook hands, and my team signed off on the last-minute details as Emery packed up her paperwork.

"You look lovely today, sweetness," I whispered lowly into her ear. Not caring if anyone saw me. Raising a hand, I gently caressed her arm, and she moved away from my touch.

"Not here, Jackson," Emery replied in aggravation and walked away from me.

Shaking hands with Brent and my team, I moved to walk out of the office to catch up with Emery. Before I could get out, Dominique blocked me from leaving.

"Thank you again for letting me lead on this project, Jackson." Dominique stepped closer into my space and seductively ran her hand down my chest.

"You're welcome. I need to take care of something. If you have any questions, you can talk with my lead counselor Gregory." I tried to step around her, and she jumped back in front of me as I noticed Emery leaving her office.

"We should celebrate with dinner. I know this cool place around where I live." Dominique pushed her breasts up against my chest. I stepped back, not wanting anyone to think we had something going on, especially if it got back to Emery.

"Sorry, I don't date," I responded and moved her hand away from my arm, walking toward the elevator. Seeing the door close, I walked toward her secretary's desk to find out her schedule for the day.

"Is Emery going to be gone for the rest of the day?"

"Yes, sir. She had a family emergency. I can take a message and have her call you back."

"I'll catch her at another time. Thanks anyway," I replied and left to catch up with Brent.

* * *

Thirty minutes later, we were sitting in the restaurant where I met Emery, eating lunch with Brent, Angela, and Dominique. How she invited herself, I had no clue. Someone should tell her about wearing loud, strong perfume from Elisabeth Arden. It made me nauseous.

"Are you enjoying your steak, Jackson?" Dominique asked, and Angela furrowed her brows in annoyance.

"It's fine. How's your salad?"

"Dry like her personality," Angela muttered under her breath. Brent nudged her to be quiet, and I tried to hold in my laugh and take a sip of my water.

"Excuse the help, Jackson. Brent's often trying to refine his side pieces by taking them out to nice restaurants. But as you can see, she still has no class," Dominique responded and rolled her eyes as Angela tried to lunge at her as Brent pulled her back.

"Bitch! I'll show you, class. At least I can keep a man," Angela grumbled and picked her fork back up to continue eating her pasta salad.

"Ladies, can we please have one meal with no craziness. We just signed an amazing deal that's going to take Jackson and my company to the next level. Babe, if you were going to act like this, you could have stayed at the shop." Brent pulled his wallet out of his pocket and placed a fifty-dollar bill down on the table.

He nudged Angela to get up, and she wouldn't move. Seeing the relationship they'd built over the past five years had me contemplating at times if Emery and I could get to that place. At times, I could sense the hurt and pain from her ex.

"Let us go, I have an early meeting to get back for at my office. Get your food to go." Brent leaned over, shook my hand, and then answered his ringing phone. Angela flipped Dominique off while Brent was distracted by a call. I held Dominique back from getting out of the booth. Finally, Brent turned around and grabbed Angela by the waist, and we both gestured with a nod to see each other later.

"I can't stand her," Dominique mumbled under her breath as she poured another glass of wine.

"What time do you need to be back to the office?" I asked Dominique as I stood to leave the restaurant and grab my driver to locate Emery.

"I can take the rest of the day off. What did you have in mind?" Dominique responded as she licked her lips and moved in, closing the space between us.

Taking a step back, I looked around the room, hoping paparazzi left before catching any innocent flirtation.

"You know what, I have a meeting I need to get to. Do you need a ride back to your office or—"

"What does she have that I don't? From what I'm seeing, you'd be upgrading with me on your arm. Just think about it, Mr. Pierce." Dominique patted my chest, tightened my tie, and leaned on her tippy toes to kiss my cheek. Watching as she bent over and grabbed her coat and purse, I couldn't help but notice through the outline of her skirt that she wasn't wearing any underwear.

Smirking in thought about how much she lacked in substance and throwing herself at me every chance she gets, made me appreciate the woman Emery was, with her beautiful smile and confidence when she walked into a room. To her long legs and little button nose, and soft chocolate skin and a taste that left me wanting her around me twenty-four seven.

I told her goodbye and left to find Emery. Dialing her number back to back, I finally got a location on her at her grandparents' home. Stepping out of the car, I looked around the quiet neighborhood with cars lined up and down the block. I stopped to tell my driver I'd be in about fifteen minutes.

Walking up to the door, I knocked and waited for someone to answer. An older gentleman wearing blue jean overalls and a white t-shirt with car oil stains and a toothpick in his mouth opened the door.

"Which one?"

"I'm sorry, which..."

"Are you here for Angela, Jordan, or my Emery? Because either way, I got a shotgun I have no problem using if you came to cause trouble."

Surprised by his statement, I raised my hand in an innocent gesture that I came in peace.

"I work with Emery and wanted to see if I could speak with her."

"She's not here right now, young man. She took her grandmother to the store." He backed away from the door, motioned for me to come inside, and offered me a seat on the couch.

"Do you know how long she's going to be out?" I

sought out as he walked out of the living room and came back with two beers and passed me one. I usually didn't drink during the afternoon but not wanting to be rude, I grabbed the Budweiser bottle and took a sip.

"How long?" he asked me after placing his bottle down on the table.

"Excuse me, sir," Bewildered by his question, I leaned back into the couch and waited for his response.

"How long have you been in love with my Emery?"

Choking on his question, I spat the contents of my beer out on my suit and the arm of the couch. He laughed, and I apologized while trying to pull my handkerchief out to clean up my mess.

"She got you bad, I see. Just like my wife Lynn, a hardheaded, stubborn woman. I chased her down for an entire six months before she finally went out on a date with me."

"We just started seeing each other. No one's at that stage yet."

"Huh... I'll let you believe that. But I can tell you that Emery's still working through her heartbreak from Anthony. So be patient, and in time, she'll come around."

Nodding in agreement, I checked the time on my watch and noticed it was getting late. Getting up to leave, I stopped at the front door closing.

"Hey, Pops. I have the ice cream you wanted. Don't tell your wife. You know how she gets when sweets come into..."

Emery walked inside and almost dropped the bag of groceries from the shock of me being in her family's home.

"Hey sweet... I mean Emery..."

"What are you doing here? The deal finalized earlier, and Dominique is running your account. If she's not working out, then I'll assign someone else to you." She walked off and took the groceries in the kitchen. I followed her after her grandfather gestured for me to do so.

"You and I both know that's not why I'm here. We need to talk." I invaded her space, and she stepped away from me. Turning toward me, she crossed her arms over her chest and furrowed her brows in anger.

"It was just sex, Jackson. Get over it. We both know you have a book full of women you can call up. I'm too grown for games and too busy to deal with back-and-forth drama that comes with your lifestyle."

Stepping closer, she put her hands up to stop me. Feeling defeated, I ran my hand across the back of my neck from the sharp pain building into a migraine at the aggravation of Emery fighting what we could have.

"I hope you change your mind. I do care for you, sweetness."

"Don't call me that," Emery snapped back in reply.

Smirking at her annoyance, I closed the distance between us. Kissing her forehead, I lingered on her peach flowery smell until noticing her grandfather still drinking his beer in the living room. I shook his hand before saying goodbye and walking out the door.

Chapter Thirteen

Brent

One Week Later
I was playing a round of three-on-three basketball with Damon, Jackson, and a few coworkers. I needed to leave the house before I strangled Angela. Ever since I told her about moving in with me, she'd been dodging my calls, and whenever I stopped by her place, she wasn't there.

Jumping up and blocking the ball out of Damon's hand, I reached out and stole it while crossing over to hit a three-pointer. Missing an easy shot like that had us down by four points, my skills were called into question.

"I see Angela's pissed you off again. What did she do this time?" Damon snapped me out of my daze with a pat on the back.

"I asked her to move in with me."

"Really, or did you just tell her you're moving in with me, and you have no choice but to do as I say." He picked up the ball and dribbled it back and forth, then passed it to Jackson as he shot a layup.

"Does it matter? She's my girl, and we've been

together for over five years. I'm getting older, and I want a wife and kids. She knew this about me," he replied after picking up the ball again and calling timeout.

"You mean on and off over five years, right?" He cocked his head to the side and wagged his eyes up and down.

"You can't be talking. Aren't you trying to get a date with Jordan, and she keeps avoiding your calls?"

He shrugged and walked off to pick up his bottled water. After he passed the other guys one, we sat on the bench and watched other families in the park playing.

"What's her story, man? I like Jordan; she's quiet and sassy at the same time. Funny, a challenge and of course beautiful. Seeing how she's raising her son alone is showing me she doesn't hide away when it gets tough." Damon asked and scratched his head after pouring water over his head to cool off.

"That's her story to tell, man. Just remember to be gentle with her. She's a cool girl, and DJ's her heart. If you want to get in with Jordan, you need DJ on your side." I informed him and picked up my keys and bag, ready to leave to find Angela.

"Cut her off, man. Women aren't worth the aggravation," Jackson sighed out in a harsh breath.

Damon, Stephen, and Camden cackled at Jackson's expense. Everyone at work knew his dilemma with Emery. I told him plenty of times to leave her alone. She was one of my best friends, but Anthony did a number on her heart. All the guys followed, and we dapped and shook hands to head toward our respective cars. Checking my phone, I saw a missed call from Angela.

Tired of chasing after her, I blocked her number and drove off. Twenty minutes later, I pulled up to my house and headed inside to change clothes. Not relishing being alone for the night, I called up an old girlfriend to see if she was up for dinner and a movie.

***

An hour later, Lauren and I parked at Sybil's restaurant for dinner. I reminded myself to ignore my feelings for Angela tonight and relax with Lauren. Knowing she was a second choice wasn't fair, but I needed to let the past go.

I placed my hand on her lower back to guide her in front of me. The hostess approached us.

"Hello, how many in your party?"

"Two please."

We followed the hostess and sat at a table in the middle of the room.

"Your waiter will be with you soon," the hostess stated and left.

"So, what made you decide to call me again, Brent? That last time we talked, you were dating that loud mouth girl who does hair for a living," Lauren stated as she set her purse down and relaxed in her chair.

After taking a sip of my water and fiddling with the menu, I decided to be honest.

"Angela and I have had an on-off relationship. Currently off at the moment—"

"Says who?" Angela said and set her hands flat on the table, leaning into my face with a pissed-off look on her face.

Seeing Lauren flinch at her intrusion, I looked between both women, trying to think of a way out of this with Lauren not getting hurt, or Angela ending up in jail from fighting.

"Lauren, can you give me a minute? I need to talk with Angela for a second."

"Whatever you have to say to me you can say in front of Lucy."

"My name is Lauren."

Angela rolled her eyes and picked up Lauren's menu, getting ready to place an order.

"Lucy, Lauren, either way, he won't need to remember. Right, Brent?" Angela gripped the arm of the chair as she narrowed her eyes at Lauren.

Feeling rage rolling through my body at Angela embarrassing me, I stood to take control of the situation. Excusing myself from Lauren, I led Angela outside to the front of the restaurant, while looking back through the window at Lauren, feeling a hint of guilt at the interruption.

"You made your decision when you didn't move in, and you've dodged all my calls. Angela, you want to be single. So, have a good life."

"Brent, baby, wait. I'm sorry. Give me a little time. You know we've been doing good for the past five years. Why change it now?"

"Because I want to have a family, and you knew this about me!" I yelled as I shook with fury at her dismissing my feelings.

"I'm not ready for that!" she shrieked and buried her face in her hands.

"Then I have no choice. I have to move on and find somebody who wants the same things that I want. We've been down this road for five years, Angela. I love you, but I need to put myself first this time." Seeing her flinch at my words, I leaned over to kiss her lips one last time before walking back in to finish my date with Lauren.

Sitting back down, Lauren looked over at me, perplexed by the situation that just happened. I took her hand and placed a kiss on it for reassurance. She seemed to relax, and we continued with our conversation.

"Sorry about that. She won't be interrupting us any further. So, tell me what have you been up to lately? Last time we talked, it was a year ago at the banquet event for my company."

"I feel we should talk about the elephant in the room. Are you sure it's over between you two? I'd rather know up front before feelings get involved," Lauren replied as the waitress brought out our food. I didn't order anything, but from the looks of things, Lauren took charge and made sure I was taken care of without knowing if I was staying or leaving with Angela.

"Since you ordered for me already, I guess you know the answer to that question." Chuckling at her blushing, we both ate and finished our date.

Chapter Fourteen

Jordan

"Angela, what did you expect him to say? You've juggled that relationship in his face for over five years." I stood to pour another glass of wine and pass the bottle to Angela, then Emery as we caught up with each other.

"He could have waited before making a huge leap like this and with that Lauren slut. Ohhh... I hate her." Angela rubbed her temples as she paced the room in anger.

"Why? Because she's going to give Brent what he wants, and you're feeling inadequate?" I questioned to hopefully get her to open up about her parents' abandonment.

Angela stopped in her tracks to turn and flip me off. She took the bottle out of Emery's hand and guzzled it down.

"Hey, I was still drinking that," Emery said and tried to take the bottle back. They're both standing and playing tug of war with a bottle of wine like two teenagers fighting over a boy.

"Really, you're both going to sit here and fight over a bottle of wine?"

"She started it." Angela drank the last of the wine and stuck her tongue out playfully.

Emery rolled her eyes and sat back down.

"How have you been, Emery? How's everything with Jackson?"

"Fine." She shrugged and picked up the remote to turn on the TV. DJ ran out of his room toward Angela and wrapped his arms around her legs.

"Auntie GiGi, can you take me to Tessa's house?"

She bent down to pick him up and playfully kissed all over his face.

"Who's Tessa, baby?" She playfully tickled him on his stomach, and he squirmed around in laughter.

Seeing the smile on his face made all the late hours' worth it, seeing him safe, fed, and happy with my family. When the weather got better, I'd visit Devin's family in Washington, so they could spend some time with him.

"Baby, you'll see Tessa tomorrow."

"She's my friend at school, Auntie, and her dad's nice too. He even took Mommy and me out for ice cream and dinner."

"Did he now? Is this mommy's friend, DJ?" Angela tried prying information out of my baby, offering him cookies and hot chocolate.

"Are you trying to give my child diabetes?"

Angela ignored my comment and continued to entertain DJ. A few minutes later, she let him down, and he ran toward me. After kissing his forehead and cheek, I sent him back to his room to play before bedtime.

"I don't want to hear it. It was just ice cream for the

kids. So, Emery, tell us about this new guy in your life Jackson Pierce, the billionaire CEO of NASCAR."

"A billionaire? Please tell me he has a brother," Angela joked, plopping down between us on the couch and picking up the bowl of popcorn.

"First off, he doesn't have a brother, and second, he's not my boyfriend."

"Will you guys go with me to TP Brent's house and take all the air out of his tires?" Angela asked with a straight face, not worried at all about getting in trouble.

"I do pray for you and the child who ends up with you as the mother. I can see it now, you stressed and calling every five minutes, needing bail money." Emery stood, stretched, grabbed her purse, and stepped back into her shoes.

"You're my best friends. What happened to ride together no matter what happens?"

"Not if it's going to end up with us in jail, I'm not. You're an adult, Angela, and decided to leave Brent hanging. He decided to teach you a permanent lesson. Either step up or move on," I informed her as I stood to gather the dishes and clean up.

"Jordan's right, Angela. Brent's been chasing you for over five years, including high school. Take some time to find out what you want and let him do the same. I must deal with Anthony popping up at my home and job every other day and Jackson barging in at my grandparents' house. Men are the last thing we need right now."

"Ohh... he lets you call him Jackson and not Mr. Pierce now?" Angela asked.

Emery stopped at the door, grabbed her jacket, and turned around with the door slightly opened.

"Mr. Pierce at work and Daddy at night." Emery winked, and we all burst into laughter at her statement.

Feeling my phone vibrate in my pocket, I waved Emery goodbye as she left and noticed Damon's name across the screen.

"Hello?"

"How are you and the little man doing tonight, beautiful?" Damon asked on the other end of the line.

Seeing Angela engrossed in the TV show, I walked toward my bedroom for some privacy.

"I'm fine, Damon. Is there something you needed?"

Hearing a grunt coming from the other end of the phone made me smile in appreciation for his efforts in putting up with me.

"Have dinner with me, just the two of us?"

"Why?"

"Because I see what you're trying to hide from, and I get it. Not that I've had someone die on me. But a loss, in general, is a tough thing to hold onto. Besides, if you have a terrible time, I'll never bother you again."

"Something tells me that's a lie."

"You're right. I'm never giving up." We burst out in laughter at his acknowledgment.

"Okay."

"Really?"

"Yes, and I'll pay for my food."

"That's never going to happen, baby."

"Ahhh, I'm baby now. It seems we're jumping ahead of ourselves, aren't we, Damon?"

"Nope, I'm just getting you used to the word."

"Anyway, I have to get off this phone and give DJ a bath before bed. I'll talk with you this weekend."

"Good night, Jordan."

"Good night, Mr. Adams."

"I see you got jokes. Okay, well, give DJ a dap for me and tell him Tessa is ready for another playdate."

"I will and thanks for being patient, Damon."

"Anything worth having is worth fighting for."

Hanging up, I checked in DJ's room and noticed he was passed out, lying on top of his bed with all his clothes still on. Not wanting to disturb him, I placed him under the covers and decided to bathe him early in the morning.

Chapter Fifteen

Emery

Six shots and two margaritas had me slowly walking into work with a hangover; not one of my best ideas. Especially with the new medication the doctor prescribed. I decided to tell my family and Jackson this week before things got further along. No telling if I had another situation with no one around to help me.

Waiting for the elevator to go upstairs, I noticed Dominique running to catch the elevator. Knowing if the shoe was on the other foot, she'd let the doors close on me. Being the bigger person, I held it open, and she surprisingly said thank you.

"Nice shoes, Emery. Are those from two seasons ago from Marc Jacobs?"

"I'm not sure, Dominique. They were a gift from my ex."

"Interesting. Well, did you hear about my date with Jackson? He couldn't keep his hands off me. I can't wait for my debut with him at the NASCAR Fantasy Fastlane Pre-race."

"I didn't hear anything about a date. Just remember Mr. Pierce is your boss at the end of the day, and you're representing Townsend Advertising. I'd hate for anything to jeopardize our chances at keeping him as a client because of a lover's quarrel."

Finally getting off on our floor, we walked off, heading in the same direction as our offices.

"Jackson said he'd be more than happy to bring a date for you if you need it. I mean it's a big event with media showing up. I think it would look bad if the vice president of his account never showed."

Reaching my office and opening the door, we both stood in shock at the room filled with flowers. Closing and opening the door again, I blinked, thinking this couldn't be real.

Dominique pushed me aside gently and walked into the room ahead of me.

"Who sent you flowers? I mean did somebody die or something?"

"What? No, of course not."

"Ohh, thank God you're finally here, Emery. I've tried to turn every delivery guy away and even sent flowers to other tenants in the building," my secretary stated.

"Ummm, do we know who they're from?"

"It says anonymous on the clipboard. Check the card and see."

Picking up the card and seeing Dominique staring, I turned with my back toward her to read the card. Seeing Jackson's name displayed I bit down on my bottom lip, thinking of a way out of this. He wanted to meet me for lunch, and if I declined, he'd meet me in person.

"So, who's the secret admirer, Emery?" Dominique

tried looking over my shoulder to sneak a peek at the note crumbled up in my hand.

"Uhhh, Brent sent them as a thank you for all the hard work the team has done on Mr. Pierce's campaign. Dominique, if you would excuse me. I need to make a call."

Watching her grab her briefcase and purse and yank my door open to walk out, I released the breath I'd been holding since we walked into my office. I decided to call Jackson to give him a piece of my mind.

Dialing his number, it went straight to voicemail. I tried again, and his voicemail popped back up. *I can't believe he's ignoring me.* I knew I was a little harsh but with everything going on in my life, I couldn't bring my baggage into a new relationship.

Deciding to talk with Brent about my problems, I placed my things down and headed over to his office before things got too busy, but then I noticed Brent escorting some woman out of his office, holding her hand.

"Hey, Emery. I'm glad you're here." Brent smiled, then extended his arm around the woman's shoulder and pulled her close into his body as though she needed protection.

"I wanted to see if we could chat for a few minutes about something personal..."

"Anthony's not bothering you again, is he?"

Ignoring Brent's question, I found myself drawn to the woman by his side. He sensed my discomfort and introduced me.

"Babe, this is Emery Stone, one of my oldest friends and VP of advertising at Townsend. Emery, this is my girlfriend Lauren Johnson."

"Hi. Nice to meet you, Emery. Brent has told me so

much about you. I feel like I've known your whole life," Lauren said as she extended her hand.

Feeling annoyance throughout my body at Brent shoving some new plaything down my throat, I plastered on a smile and shook her hand.

"I wish I could say the same for you, Lauren. Unfortunately, Brent's been keeping you hidden from his close friends since middle school."

"Emery, it's not like that. We dated a year ago and just reconnected a few weeks ago. Let me walk her to the elevator, and I'll meet you in my office." Brent walked off with Lauren following him.

Ten minutes later, he walked back in with a look of guilt and aggravation from me peering into his eyes. He threw his hands in the air, moved toward the bar in his office, and poured himself a glass of whiskey. To be drinking at nine in the morning told me he was under some stress.

"Don't look at me like that, Emery. It was her choice," Brent said as he downed the drink and poured another one.

"Can you blame her, Brent? You forced her to choose, and you know she doesn't like when anybody tries to control her. You of all people know she has abandonment issues."

"I... I... can't keep doing this dance with her. We've been on and off for over five years, eight if you include high school."

Seeing the pain Brent was going through had me rethinking talking to him about Jackson. Taking a seat next to him on the couch, I grabbed the glass out of his hand and took a sip of his drink.

"Ewww... that's disgusting." I spat out the contents of

the alcohol while choking. Brent took the glass out of my hand and laughed softly.

"That's what you get for doing big boy things."

"Whatever. Have you seen her lately? I know she's been working overtime at the shop, and you know the anniversary of her being with the family is coming up. She needs all of us, Brent."

"No."

"Hear me out. I'm not saying you have to take her out or anything, but the family is throwing a little party for her to celebrate. We do this every year, and she wants you there."

"I doubt that after the last time we spoke. I left her standing outside and went back to my date." Brent stood, placed the glass down on the table, and walked over to his desk.

"Yeah, I was hanging with Jordan at her place when Angela stormed inside and told us. What the hell are you doing with Lauren of all people? Last time we talked, you said she's a stuck-up princess who doesn't do oral sex."

"Oral sex isn't everything that matters to me, Emery. I'm getting older... hell, we're all getting older. We're reaching thirty, and Angela's never going to change. I've shown her every part of me and supported anything she wanted or needed. All I ask is to be a family in return."

I stood, and we embraced before going back to work. "Angela is different."

"Give her some time. She'll figure out what she wants." Leaving his office, I decided to try one more time to call Jackson.

After finishing my conversation with Brent and settling back in at my office, I tried dialing Jackson's number. Before the phone could ring, a text message popped up. Thinking it could be Jackson, I hung up and checked. *Who's Jessica?*

Jackson's friend Jessica: Thought you'd like to know our man's available for everyone.

I felt a punch in my stomach seeing a picture of Jackson, in bed with another woman with the sheet only covering his lower half. I know I shouldn't be pissed but noticed the time stamp was two days ago when he took Dominique out. Furious was the safest word I could use for right now.

Me: You have me confused with someone else. Stop playing childish games on my phone. Oh... and tell Jackson he can go fuck himself.

Switching my phone to vibrate, I checked messages and caught up on some work I'd neglected for the past few days.

Later that night, I decided to call the girls over to drink and vent about their problems.

"Angela, don't you have a key?" I asked as I opened the door to let her and Jordan inside. Both were dressed in pajamas, carrying bottles of wine. I grabbed one out of her hand and used the wine opener from the table.

"So, who broke your heart and how much is it going to cost me?" Angela questioned as she plopped down next to me on the couch, placing her feet on the coffee table.

"Check my cell phone."

Angela scrolled through my messages as Jordan came behind the couch and looked over her shoulder.

"Did you ask him if this is real? You know how people photoshop stuff," Jordan said.

"He's not my man. I could care less what he does."

Angela rolled her eyes and texted on my phone.

"What are you doing?" I asked.

"Texting Jackson about this photo." Angela stood and walked to the kitchen.

"Don't text him; I'd rather not deal with his excuses."

"Too late, he said to call him," Angela said.

Waving off her suggestion, I turned the TV on as Jordan laid her head in my lap.

"What's your problem, Jordan?"

"Trying to decide if I should go out with Damon on a real date. After we made the whole family dinner with the kids, he persuaded me to a one on one," Jordan replied as she sat back up again to take the bottle and chug some down.

"He must have made an impression on you."

"I shouldn't be dating. DJ would get confused, and I can't have him getting attached to anyone, only to end up getting hurt in the long run," Jordan said.

"Jordan, you're thinking too hard about this. It's only one date. DJ only cares about cookies and pizza right now. I doubt he even remembers his name," Angela replied.

I took the bottle out of her hand and poured some into my glass just as someone rang the doorbell.

Chapter Sixteen

Jackson

I was annoyed about Jessica setting me up and Emery walking away at the first sign of trouble. Standing outside her apartment in the middle of the night to discuss Jessica's handy work with the media wasn't my idea of a nightly visit.

"Emery, open the door."

"Go away, Jackson!" Emery shouted from the other side of the door. Ringing the bell and knocking louder, I suddenly heard the locks turning and saw the door opening to reveal Angela standing with her arms crossed and an icy glare in her eyes.

"I was hoping you didn't turn into a douchebag like Brent," Angela said as she let me pass by into the apartment.

"I was set up, Angela. Everyone knows I can't stand Jessica."

"Huh, could have fooled me," Emery said as she walked closer and stood in front of me with short silk pajama pants and bunny slippers on her feet.

"Nice slippers, sweetness."

As I grabbed her hand, she stepped back and shook her head, causing a sharp sting in my chest from the rejection.

"Hear me out."

"I've seen enough. Have a nice life with Jessica and whoever else you've been seeing," she said, walking down the hall toward her bedroom.

Jordan and Angela both shook their heads as they left.

"Give her a little space. When she gets like this, it's best to steer clear. Emery tends to get disrespectful," Jordan informed me before she walked out.

"I say just put her to sleep with some good dic—"

Jordan yanked Angela out of the door mid-sentence, and I watched as both girls bickered back and forth toward their cars.

Debating on having a conversation or not with Emery weighed heavily on my mind, along with her fainting the other day in my presence. She passed it off as being dehydrated. Tonight, I'd give her a pass. Tomorrow, we'd have a conversation and lay everything out on the table. Heading to her bedroom, I noticed for the first time the cream-colored walls with hanging African art pieces and some quotes by Tony Morrison hanging on the wall.

Standing in her bedroom doorway, I took in the large king-size bed with baby-blue sheets and gold posts with ropes across each railing. Seeing Emery under the covers with the sheet pulled over her head, I took off my shoes and jacket. Pulling the sheets back, I crawled in bed and wrapped my arms around her. She tensed at my touch.

"Why are you still here?" she mumbled under her breath.

I kissed her shoulder and moved her closer to me. "Go to sleep, sweetness."

We both fell asleep together. In the morning, we'd discuss both our exes and the latest scam to get me back.

* * *

Eight hours later, we arrived at my NASCAR race track. I decided to bring her here so she couldn't run away from me, and we could keep all the outside noise away while having breakfast.

"Have you ever seen a race up close, Emery?" I asked as she jumped out of the passenger-side door, being stubborn once again.

"No, and I wasn't planning on it today. Jackson, you're going to try to sweet talk me by waving your money around."

"I'm hungry, and we have a meeting scheduled this week anyway, so we can just have it right now," I said as we walked into the main building, heading to the outside field.

"Is this how you got Jessica to fall in love with you?"

"Emery, today is about you. Jessica lied and sent you those photos to make it seem like we slept together recently."

"Huh..."

Shaking hands with my field agent and seeing my personal chef here, I wrapped my arms around Emery and kissed her soft lips.

"Today is a beautiful day. Please hear me out, Emery, before you completely cut me off."

"Depends."

Assisting Emery with her chair to sit, and I took the seat across from her. I could sense the awkward and harsh tone of how our breakfast would be.

"Depends on what?"

"On how good this food turns out."

Chuckling at her response, I leaned over, and she met me halfway for a kiss on her soft, plump lips. I thought about her other set of lips that I couldn't wait to have for dinner. Already I could feel my dick putting a tent in my pants.

Chapter Seventeen

Jordan

"Anthony, I don't have time to fool with you, and if Teresa pisses me off one more time, I'll have to knock her out for disrespecting mommy and daddy."

"Jordan, call her for me, and I won't bother you again. I apologized a million times. What more can I do?" Anthony stood in front of me, pacing back and forth in my living room.

It was eight in the morning, and I'd just dropped DJ off at school. I lingered around the building in hopes I would see Damon, but the teacher said his daughter was sick, so she stayed home. Now I was dealing with my brother coming over for me to call Emery and set up a meeting for him to talk with her. Somehow, he was convinced he could woo her back into his good graces and forget about his cheating with her ex-best friend.

"Anthony, stop pacing. You're giving me a headache."

"What do you think I should do about Teresa?"

I scowled at the mention of the witch who used to be one of my closet friends.

"I don't know... marry her, I guess? Emery's not taking you back."

"That's not helpful, Jordan. I made a mistake, and now my best friend's turned against me." Anthony laid his head back on the couch with his arms across his face.

"Are you crying?"

"What? No, Jordan. Damn."

"I'm just checking. Anyway, I have things to do, and one is meeting with a client and lunch with Mommy. So, are you staying or going?"

Feeling defeated, he stood, pulled his keys from his pocket, and kissed me on the cheek while walking to the door.

"I do love her, Jordan," he somberly said.

"That's what makes this so difficult, Anthony. We all thought you loved Emery since you were little kids. But you let Teresa get her claws into you, and now look at where you are... miserable with a crazy baby mamma and the love of your life moving on with someone else."

Nodding in agreement, Anthony shut my door, and I picked up my phone, noticing a text message from Damon.

Damon: Sorry I missed you today.

Me: It's okay. I heard your little girl's sick.

Damon: She's got a cold, sleeping right now. Let me take you out to dinner.

Me: Maybe

Damon: That's a yes?

Me: Maybe

Smirking at his last remark, I placed my phone back in my bag and headed out to run some errands.

Chapter Eighteen

Jackson

"Mr. Pierce, you have a call from Brent Townsend on line three," my secretary said.

"Thanks, put him through."

"Man, you need to do something about Jessica. She's all over the blogs, talking about you guys getting married and how she made a mistake," Brent said in a rush.

"Everyone knows Jessica's a liar. You give her too much attention, then she runs with it. Ignore her, and she'll give up eventually. Emery is my only concern right now."

"How are things going with her after all this broke in the media?"

"She ignored my calls after we had breakfast the other morning. I spent the night with her, and the next morning she dodged me."

I ran a hand down my face in frustration at the mess my PR was having to clean up over a girl I haven't dated in over a year or two.

"Give her some time. I saw her briefly, and then she

made up some excuse of not feeling well and went home sick."

I leaned up in my chair at the mention of Emery being sick. "Brent, let me ask you a question and be honest with me."

"Of course, we're friends. I have no reason to lie."

"Is Emery sick or have you known her to be sick in the past?"

"No, why do you ask?" Brent inquired.

"Not sure. Just seems like whenever she's in my presence, she seems to fall ill."

"Maybe she's just sick and tired of you," Brent joked.

"Says the guy who dated the same girl on and off for over five years and never got a commitment," I replied jokingly.

"Whatever. Emery, as far as I know, is fine. It's probably her period or something."

"Yeah, you may be right. Anyway, let me get back to work, and I'll call you later. Are you guys coming out to the opening races?"

"Yep, and it would look nice if you and Dominique can get along and maybe take some photos together."

"I'm fine; it's your girl who's always throwing herself at me. You'd think after I turned her down, she'd get the memo that I'm not interested."

"I'll talk with Dominique and tell her to keep it respectful. Just be nice, and we won't have any problems," Brent told me and hung up.

Feeling annoyed at Emery avoiding me all morning and yesterday, I decided it was time we came to an agreement about what we were doing. I buzzed my secretary to let her know I was leaving for the day.

"Yes, Mr. Pierce?"

"Hold all my calls unless it's an emergency; also reschedule my meetings. I'm leaving for the day and won't be back until tomorrow."

"Yes, Mr. Pierce."

The growl of my stomach had me parking in front of Sybil's. Not hearing back from Emery and dealing with the bullshit from Jessica and the media, I was falling off my game. For many years, I had made sure my company, employees, and I were always away from the gossip. Now facing an onslaught of questions and photos that Jessica released without my consent had me fuming.

* * *

For the next few days, I decided to try to lay low. I walked inside and greeted the hostess.

"How many in your party, Mr. Pierce?"

"Just me, Linda. Is Sybil here tonight?"

She picked up one menu and motioned for me to follow her. Hearing a laugh in the room that sounded so familiar, I looked and couldn't believe my eyes. Emery was sitting with a client that I was still thinking of signing a deal with. From our first meeting, Anthony Davis came across as slimy, cocky, and underhanded. I didn't care what her reasoning for sitting with his ass was. Emery wouldn't be another notch on his belt.

Emery must have felt me watching. We made eye contact and if I had my gun, her date would be one dead, self-centered jackass. Storming over, I yanked her out of the seat and placed her behind me. Then I proceeded to punch Anthony.

"Jackson!" Emery shrieked out.

"Stay away from her!" I shouted and tried to wrap my hand around Emery's wrist, but she jerked away.

"No, it's not what you think," Emery shouted.

"Emery, who is he to you?" Anthony motioned his hand at me.

"Don't worry about it, Anthony." Emery groaned, picked up her purse, and rushed out of the restaurant.

Chapter Nineteen

Emery

I paced the living floor, trying to decide the next step in my conflict to tell Jackson about my health update. I didn't expect him to show up at the restaurant tonight though. I could imagine the hurt he must have felt seeing me with Anthony. What he didn't know was that I needed closure. What Anthony and Teresa did hurt me to my core.

Bang! Bang! Bang!

"Open this door, Emery, before I break it down!"

Maybe I could turn the lights off and pretend to be asleep.

"The longer you wait, the worst it'll be!"

"Go away, Jackson! You said enough tonight at dinner."

"Sweetness, please open the door. I was wrong to treat you like that, and I apologize."

"Just go home and sleep it off."

"No!"

Hearing him kick my door, I rushed to open it and let him inside.

"Are you crazy? You're going to wake the entire neighborhood!"

Jackson stalked inside and held me against the wall. Shit, I needed to calm down before I ripped his clothes off. I worked to tame my breathing with his body heat up close and keep my juices from flowing at seeing him be possessive tonight. His soft hands tenderly caressed along my jaw. Fuck it, meeting him halfway for a kiss, I tightened my grip around his neck as he lowered his hands on top of his favorite place, my ass.

"No, Jackson. I can't do this with you. You hurt me tonight."

After giving up the fight and falling into his arms, he finally put me on my feet, and I walked to the kitchen. I opened the fridge to grab a bottle of water for us both.

"Sweetness, I refuse to let you walk out of my life. I apologize for acting out of character with you at the restaurant, but you shouldn't have lied to me."

He removed his jacket and placed it on the couch. I noticed a dark, round mark on his neck. Moving in closer, I gripped his chin to turn his head toward me. He jerked away from my touch.

"Nice hickey."

"What are you talking about?"

"Tell your little girlfriend to ease up next time, or my shoe might leave a permanent mark."

I stomped off to the bedroom, leaving him to mumble behind my back and follow. He gripped my elbow gently and pulled me close to his chest.

"Let me go."

"Baby, she didn't mean anything to me."

"I could care less. We're not in a relationship. Remember, this was a long one-night stand."

I jerked away and walked into the bedroom to grab my things for bed.

"Emery, don't walk away like this. Besides, I've played by your rules for the last few days. Now you're going to talk to me."

"Excuse me?"

"I said we have unfinished business to talk about."

Jackson came around and walked in closer, taking my nightgown and robe out of my hands. He placed them back on the dresser and stood to lean across from me with his arms folded.

"You can't fix this with sex, Jackson."

"I'm not trying to, sweetness."

"Ohhh..."

Trailing his hands down to the edge of my skirt, he ran his hand along the hem and inserted one finger into my pussy.

"What are you doing?"

"I need you, sweetness."

Shaking off his seduction, I pulled away and headed toward the bathroom. "I can't be what you need. It wouldn't be fair to either one of us."

I could hear his frustration from the harsh breath he blew as I turned and checked the water temperature in the shower.

"Emery, I'm not him. I wouldn't do that to you. What we've shared is special, and I'm not letting you go."

"I know you wouldn't cheat on me, Jackson. We just got swept away, and there are moments I'll always cherish and remember. You're technically my boss, and I don't want to be known for getting a raise because I slept with the CEO and scored his account."

"Do I look like an idiot to you, Emery?"

"Huh?"

"I know this has nothing to do with your job or Anthony. So, stop lying and be honest about why you're so against us being together."

I sighed and removed my clothes. Stepping into the shower, I tried to avoid his lingering stares.

"What are you doing?"

Jackson removed his shoes and unzipped his pants. Taking off his shirt, I tried not to look at how his defined muscles and chest hair led to his long, thick dick. I wanted another taste of him. Fighting back temptation, I ignored him as he stood in the shower. He took the rag and soap out of my hands and washed my back.

"Sweetness, one thing you'll learn about me is that I don't give up. Especially when it's something I want, and Emery, I want your mind, body, and soul."

Pulling him to my chest, I nuzzled his neck as we fell into each other like two people who haven't seen each other in a long time.

Chapter Twenty

Jackson and Emery

Lying between her legs, I ran my tongue up and down her thighs, stimulating her bud. I intended to make her fall in love with me again and again until the thought of not being in my life caused her conflict. Flicking her nipples, I kept her on edge with changing up my pace from slowly sucking to biting down roughly. I could never get enough of her chocolate drops. These past few days, I realized I couldn't even sleep without her at night and not because of the sex. It was just who she was and how she made me feel.

"Mmmm... Jackson, right there."

Slowly kneading her breasts, I wanted to get her worked up to where she couldn't deny what we had and how good it could be. She clung to my shoulders as I moved down to her slit. I flicked my tongue over her wetness. Her sweetness tasted like peaches and lingered on my tongue.

"Jackson, stop torching me."

"Baby, I'm nowhere near torching you yet," I replied.

Gripping her cheeks, I moved lower and dipped my tongue into her tight hole. Next time, we'd explore my favorite part on her body.

"We have dinner reservations, remember?"

"I remember, and we'll make them; just let me have you."

"Fuck... Emery, you taste so good, baby."

"Let me taste you."

"Next time...Damn, you're wet."

Positioning her legs on my shoulders, I slipped into her tight core. I dipped my head lower and gently kissed her cheek, ear, and nose. She arched her back, meeting me thrust for thrust. Feeling her soft hands rubbing up and down my back, in a circular motion, a shiver ran through my body as my thrusts quickened. Her smell of peaches engulfed the room, and I raised my hips up and slammed into her harder.

"Jacksonnnn! I swear..."

"Are you leaving me, Emery?"

"No, baby, no," she whimpered and leaned up to kiss my lips.

She clung to my shoulders and tightened her legs around my hips. I could feel the room spinning and sweat pouring off my face and onto her breasts and stomach. Emery grabbed my chin and darted her tongue into my mouth. We fought for control and all of a sudden, she convulsed in my arms, and her eyes rolled into the back of her head.

"Emery... Emery. Baby, say something."

Pulling out of her, I turned her on her side and checked her pulse. It was faint. I grabbed the phone on the nightstand and called 911.

"911. What your is emergency?" the operator asked.

"I need an ambulance at 3569 Malcolm Lane. Hurry, she has a faint pulse."

I was still attempting to wake Emery when I heard a knock at her door. "Fuck, baby, please wake up."

Rushing to throw on my boxers and pants, I walked out of her bedroom and opened the front door for the ambulance.

"What are you doing here?"

"I'm sorry, Jackson. I still love her," Anthony stated and pushed his way inside.

Not feeling up to fighting at this moment, I ran back into the bedroom and left him in the living room.

"Emery, baby, wake up."

Lightly tapping her across the face, I tried to wake her. Anthony rushing into the bedroom didn't help the situation.

"What the fuck!" Anthony shouted and moved toward Emery lying in my arms.

"Get the fuck out," I glared as I tried to keep my emotions under control.

"I'm not leaving her. What did you do to her? I knew I shouldn't have left her alone."

Right before I was about to knock Anthony out, the paramedics rushed into the room and lifted Emery out of my arms. Checking her pulse and vitals, I leaned in closer to make sure no one hurt her.

"What happened to her?" the paramedic questioned as he placed an oxygen mask on her face.

"We were in bed and all of a sudden, she passed out," I responded, not giving the exact details of us having sex. Maybe I was a little too rough with her this time.

"Is that all you were doing, just sleeping?"

Anthony glared at Emery lying on the floor naked; it made me want to protect her even more.

"We were in the middle of having sex."

"You son of a bitch! Leave her alone!" Anthony tried to push around the other paramedic and hit me. By this time, the police had arrived.

"Sir, are you related to her at all?" he asked Anthony as they kept us separated.

"She's my fiancée, and we'd just gotten back together," Anthony lied, trying to get out of the police officer's arms.

"You'll both have to ride separately to the hospital. I can't have you stressing our patient."

Grabbing my shoes and shirt, I picked up my keys and grabbed my cell to call Brent and Emery's friends to meet me at the hospital.

* * *

Emery

"Emery, Granny loves you, and even though you get your stubborn ways from your grandfather, I need you to wake up and talk to us, baby."

Hearing the voices of my family and friends in the room, I continued going in and out of a deep sleep. I had been stressed because Jackson and I were not talking, and I'd seen him all over the news with different women. His company was also launching with our new ads, so he had been working overtime, avoiding my calls and messages. I couldn't remember the number of times I'd driven to his office. Kimberly, feeling sorry for me, had even tried to get him to hear me out.

Two days later.

Sitting up in the hospital bed, eating breakfast, Angela and Jordan came inside.

"Sleeping beauty is awake," Angela joked and walked inside, wrapping her arms around me for a hug.

"Emery, why didn't you tell us? We've been your best friends for over twenty years. I can't believe you kept something like lupus from me," Jordan said before placing her purse down and picking DJ up to sit in her lap.

"I'm sorry, Jordan and Angela. I guess I just thought if I kept it to myself, I could handle it alone and not burden anyone with my problems."

"Emery, if you weren't like a sister to me, I would kick your ass all up and through this hospital," Angela responded.

"How are things with Jackson? I know he was here with you when they brought you in with Anthony right behind him. How did that work out?" Jordan inquired.

"Not good. They both almost ended up getting arrested. He hates me and thinks I'm back with your dumbass brother. He sat up here telling the doctors we're engaged."

"I can handle Anthony, but what are you going to do about Jackson? You need to apologize to him and your family. Your parents were so upset and thought Angela and I knew all along," Jordan told her.

"We spoke over the phone, and they'll be up here in a few minutes. Jackson's my only priority at the moment. I should be getting discharged soon. Can you hand me my purse, Angela?"

When Angela handed it over to me, I pulled my phone out to call Jackson.

Dialing his number, it went straight to voicemail.

"Can you get the doctor for me, Angela?"

"Maybe you should give him some space before you go and talk to him. It's not like you didn't just keep your illness from him."

Chapter Twenty-One

Emery

A few days later.

Staying out in the country, away from the hustle and bustle of the city, I'd finally gotten my strength back. The night I passed out in Jackson's arms still replayed in my mind.

He still wasn't taking my calls, and my friends stayed with me around the clock ever since I told them about being diagnosed with lupus. My parents and grandparents hadn't left the house unless it was to check on their homes back in the city. But the only person I was missing was Jackson, and he refused to talk with me.

"Girl, are you still sitting up in this room, looking depressed over your baby daddy?"

Yep, the night I passed out, the doctor told me I was pregnant. One month, soon to be two. I estimated the second night Jackson and I had sex, it had to have happened. It was a total shock to everyone, including myself. Even though I had this diagnosis, I refused to get rid of my child, especially since its father had blocked me out of his life.

"Angela, please don't start." I rolled my eyes as I rose out of bed to grab my robe and slippers.

"Emery, you need to get over it. This stress is not good for the baby. Besides, Jackson's not thinking about you. Have you not seen the tabloids lately? Dominique doesn't let that man breathe for nothing." Angela followed me as I walked down the stairs into the kitchen where my grandmother and mother were cooking breakfast.

"Sweet pea. how are you feeling?" Granny asked as she poured syrup on the pancakes and passed me a plate.

"I'm fine, Granny. Just ready to get back home. I know the doctor told me to stay off my feet for a few weeks, but honestly, I feel fine. I need to call Brent," I reminded myself and ate the pancakes, catching the stares from everyone looking at each other and not saying anything.

"What is it? Why do you guys look like you lost a puppy or something?"

My mother cleared her throat, and Angela placed her hand on her shoulder to interrupt what she was about to say.

"Brent split all your accounts with Dominique and Teresa." Angela stepped closer and grabbed the plate from in front of me.

Feeling a hot sensation come over me, I dropped the fork and rushed to the trashcan and threw up.

"Emery, don't let this get to you, please. Your father and I would like for you to live with us during your pregnancy. We can turn your old room into a nursery. This situation with your job can wait. You have savings, and Brent will give you your accounts back once you've rested up," Mother responded as she walked over and rubbed my back as early morning breakfast and last night's tacos spilled out.

"Stop babying that girl. Angela, start her bath water, and Elisabeth, I need you to check on your father and take his plate. Let me talk to Emery alone." Granny pointed her finger toward the living room for everyone to leave.

"He gave my accounts away to two of the least qualified people at that company. I'm going to kill him and then bring him back to kill him again." Picking up the wet towel out of her hand, I scrubbed the last remnants of vomit from my mouth and washed my hands before sitting back down.

"Are you done yet?"

"Huh..."

"I said are you done playing the victim yet?"

"Granny, I've never played the victim—"

Holding her hand up to stop me from talking, I waited for a slap or curse to come out. Anything would make me feel better compared to the hell of losing my job and man all within the same month.

"Sweet pea, you're my angel. My only grandchild, well, that I know about anyway."

"Really..."

"Hush, don't interrupt. You've held in a lot of information from your family and friends for over three months, dealt with a breakup from a guy who was never good for you in the first place. Then you meet this tall, dark, and handsome man with a big—"

"Granny! Please refrain from saying big toward any man when you're with me."

Shrugging her shoulders, she kissed me on the cheek and squeezed both hands.

"You have made a pile of shit with no plan on how to

clean it up, baby. Now I love you more than anything in the world and will fight till the death for you. Also, when you're wrong, I will tell you so. I'm not Angela, Jordan, or your mom. I keep it real, and the repercussions of you not telling us you've been sick this whole time has hurt your mother, father, and grandfather's feelings."

"I know." I lowered my head in shame at being scolded like a five-year-old for taking too many cookies.

"Do you? From what I see, you've only managed to accomplish being selfish. Emery, this doesn't have to be the end of your story. Baby, many people live with this disease and lead productive lives. Now the situation with your job... Brent had every right to find a replacement for you. That man's business must run nonstop, and if his top executive can't run the show, then he needs to find a replacement."

"I just wish it was anyone but them," I whined in her arms, leaning my head into her chest.

"Brent's coming by tomorrow, and we can talk then. He's excited to see you. He's been worried about you, Emery."

"Wait, he's coming over tomorrow?"

Nodding her head, I jumped off the stool to run upstairs to pack and leave.

"Emery... Emery... Why are you running!" my mother shrieked, following me as I rushed up the stairs.

"Because Brent's coming and more than likely he's going to tell Jackson about me." Rushing into the closet, I picked up my luggage and pulled clothes off the rack and stuffed them into my bag. I rushed to the bathroom, picking up the shampoo, lotion, and my toothbrush, tossing everything inside as fast as possible.

"Emery, you've known Brent almost your entire life.

He would never betray your trust. Besides, you're grounded. You've lied to this family for over three months, dealing with something like this alone..."

I noticed the tears pool into her eyes and fall onto her cheek. I pulled her into my arms to reassure her that this wouldn't take her little girl away from her.

Releasing her, I wiped the tears away before we moved to the bed to sit.

"Mom, I'm sorry for keeping you in the dark. That was never my intention with anyone in the family. I guess I needed time to come to grips with what the doctors told me." Wrapping my arms around her shoulders from behind, I placed a gentle kiss on her cheek.

"Emery, you're my only child, well, next to crazy Angela. You're my favorite," she joked.

Nudging her shoulders playfully, we smiled at each other. I stood from the bed to continue packing my clothes as we finished our conversation.

"Please don't tell Angela that. Her emotions are all over the place with Brent moving on to another woman and not showing up to her anniversary party."

"Soon, you'll be a mom with all the stress that comes with it, no matter how old you get. Now you're wrong for keeping your family in the dark about this and for not telling Jackson he's going to be a father."

"I know, but he's the one who shut me out. I tried to call him and sent word through his friends to call me. This isn't something to just blurt out and expect him to fall in love with me."

"Normally. you wouldn't give it up on the first date, and this wouldn't have happened," she commented as I placed the last piece of clothing into my bag.

Closing the suitcase, we headed back downstairs to

finish having dinner with the family. Following her, I escaped toward the living room to talk with my grandfather.

"Sweet pea, look at you. How are you feeling? I know the little man is causing a ruckus in there." He rubbed my stomach as I sat next to him on the couch. I wondered if I'd ever a moment like this with Jackson one day. As soon as the thought came to mind, I released it from my heart. He made his decision to walk out of my life, and I honestly couldn't blame him.

"What's the matter?" Grandfather turned from the television to look at me as I tried to get my thoughts together.

"Just thinking about the mess I've caused everyone. Jordan's still mad, and Angela ignores the issue altogether. I know she feels like I'm slowly slipping away from her and not to mention Brent putting me on an early vacation and letting Dominique and Teresa take over my accounts." Just the thought of everything coming to light caused a migraine to come on. Leaning on his shoulder, he motioned for me to put my feet up on the other side of the couch and lay in his arms.

"Sweet pea, did I ever tell you the time your grandmother and I broke up?" Shaking my head, he released a long sigh as we sat and waited on the food.

"Many moons ago, your grandmother was what you children nowadays call a thot." Laughing at his wording, I looked up into his eyes, and he kissed the top of my forehead and helped me lie back down.

"Your grandmother wasn't always this homebody, wife, mother, and grandmother to you all. We've had our ups and downs, we love each other, and no one can break that bond. Now, this young fellow came to our house and wanted to do right by you and get to know your family. You decided to shut him out if I recall." He chuckled to himself.

"Stubborn just like your grandmother, I left her after I caught her with another man."

"What?"

"Not like that, Em. She was out on a date and lied to me. Thought she was at work the whole time. A few fellows and I went out for drinks one night, and I saw her across the room with some man. Of course, he wasn't fine like your grandfather."

"Granny really played the field back then, and you forgave her?" I gasped and leaned up to look into his eyes for confirmation.

He nodded and turned his head back to the television as the New York Knicks played the Los Angeles Lakers.

"Don't tell her I told you about this. She hasn't forgiven herself, and every year, she apologizes on our anniversary. I tell her all was forgiven once she married me, but you know your grandmother is as stubborn as a mule."

"I agree with that but what made you finally decide to forgive her."

"I loved her, simple as that."

"That's it?"

"Yep. You see, Emery, you've let the outcome of your relationship with Anthony determine how you base all relationships. Sweet pea, if you haven't heard, all men are dogs." We burst into laughter at his statement as he placed a lock of my hair behind my ear.

"Anthony and I were together for so long, and he just up and betrayed me with my best friend. We were supposed to have gotten married and had kids by now."

"He was never meant to be your one constant."

"Constant what?"

"Constant person in your life who will be there with you for the good and bad. How many times have you bailed that boy out of trouble or helped him graduate high school and college? Sweet pea, this is hard to hear, but you allowed this to happen."

"No, I didn't." I glared in annoyance that everyone kept blaming me for Anthony's problems.

"Emery, your heart is big, but you're very naive with people. He walked all over you, and once you allow someone to take advantage of you, they will continue that treatment. No, I'm not saying Anthony is a bad person, but he needed to grow up. Basing every man on Anthony's actions is not right."

"I... I wasn't—"

"Girl, you're just like your grandmother. If you want to love and be loved, then you need to let go of that heart. Now let us go into the kitchen and see if my baby finished cooking."

Standing and picking up his cane, my grandfather and I joined hands, and we walked into the kitchen as my mom and grandmother finished placing the mashed potatoes and green beans in a dish.

"Ohh... you decided to grace us with your presence, Emery." Grandmother smirked as she turned the oven off and passed the bowl of gravy to my mother and walked over to kiss my grandfather on the cheek.

"Not today, Granny. Your husband already checked me for pushing Jackson away," I whined as I sat on the stool in the kitchen.

Waving me off, she sat next to me, and Grandpa sat to

the left of her, while Mom and Dad sat at the heads of the table.

"So, what are your plans after your vacation, Emery?" Dad asked as he placed a fork full of green beans into his mouth.

Taking a sip of water and placing it back down, I heard the front door opening and closing. Angela walked in with a man I'd never seen before. He was handsome, I could tell you that. He was tall, with lean muscles, high cheekbones, and a chiseled jawline. He wore a plain black shirt with the first few buttons open, showcasing his chest hair. Angela's dating a model.

"Hey, family, what's for dinner?" Angela sauntered over to grab a plate and sit to eat.

"Who's your friend, Angela?" I questioned.

"A friend. Family, this is Robert. Baby, this is my family," Angela replied as she passed Robert his plate of food.

"Robert, I'm Angela's grandmother. I know you've just met this family today, but one thing I should tell is that Angela can be a little sneaky sometimes—"

"Granny!" Angela and I yelled at the same time.

Shrugging her shoulders, she continued to eat, not caring about her little slip-up.

"Brent's on his way, Angela."

"Okay."

"When was the last time you've seen him?"

"The night you came over to Jordan's place to talk about Jackson and Dominique. He's moved on, and so have I." I peered at her as she leaned into Robert and kissed his lips like there was no one else in the room. Everyone at the table rolled their eyes at the fake display Angela was putting on.

Chapter Twenty-Two

Jackson and Emery

few days later

Staring into Emery's eyes, all the hurt and pain of our so-called relationship or lack thereof had been eye opening for me. She lied about being sick this whole time, not only to me but her family as well. I refused to soothe her. Hearing from her doctor that she'd not been taking care of herself and taking her medication, pissed me off even more.

"You need to leave," I said.

"Jackson, please just listen to me."

"I've tried to get you to listen and fight for what we have— sorry, could have. But you've got all the answers, Emery. I'm done putting in the effort. Go back to your lying, cheating ex and put up with his shit."

I turned away from her to hold onto some semblance of strength. She walked closer, pressing her front to my back and wrapped her arms around my chest. Wanting to comfort at the same time keep my distance was a hard fight between my head and heart.

"Don't throw away what we could have. I made a

mistake. This entire situation had me doubting myself, and Anthony's a non-factor in my life. I only went to dinner to make sure he understood I'd moved on from him."

Chuckling at her comment, I turned around and moved her arms away from me.

"You're so selfish, Emery. You should have put him out of your life months ago and not continue to take his calls and meet him for little dinners. Anthony wouldn't have felt so compelled to be in your presence constantly. Admit it, you still love him."

I stood my ground when I saw the tears pool into her eyes, holding back from touching and kissing them away.

"It wasn't like that, Jackson. I've known him and his family since I was a little kid. We grew up together—"

"I don't give a fuck!" I shouted, getting right in her face, as my breathing increased. She jumped back, scared.

"Don't leave me," she whimpered lowly.

Walking over to have a seat on my couch, I grabbed the remote and kicked my feet up on the table, ignoring her presence in my house. She looked at me as tears rolled down her cheek onto her shirt. Finally getting the hint that I was done talking, Emery grabbed her purse and keys to leave. I wanted to question her more about the other day and passing out, but my anger was at a level I knew we'd both end up hurt and hating each other.

* * *

Emery

Not wanting to go home alone, I headed over to Jordan and Angela's house to clear my head. Parking in her driveway and knocking on the door, I could hear DJ yelling about someone's at the door right as Jordan opened it.

"How did it go?" Jordan asked as she stood aside for me to walk in as DJ ran to hug me. I picked him up and hugged him close to my body.

"He doesn't want me anymore."

Sitting on the floor with DJ, he resumed to watch Nickelodeon cartoons and play with his Superman toys. I removed my jacket, and Jordan took it out of my hands and hung it up on the coat rack.

"Are you staying for dinner? I made stuffed chicken, green beans, cornbread, and yams."

"Yep, my family's pissed at me, along with Brent. Basically, I'm on an extended vacation from work." I fell back onto the couch and ran my hands through my hair. Feeling lost and overwhelmed with everything being out of control, I attempted once again to redial Jackson's number, and Jordan snatched my phone out of my hands.

"Give him some space. I told you about men like Jackson. You need to let them have a moment to deal with the situation. He'll talk when he's ready."

"Jordan, you're the last person who should be giving advice." Angela walked into the living room from the back and plopped down next to me.

"Coming from the woman who had a great guy and still ended up losing him because she can't admit she's in love." Jordan rolled her eyes, tucked my phone into her back pocket of her pants, and walked into the kitchen.

"She's bitchy without having any dick in her life," Angela joked as she laid her head on my shoulder, I raised my hand to push her off me. We started to play fight, and Jordan ran back inside to smack us both on the back of the head for messing around.

"Both of you need to chill out. Y'all are worse than DJ and his friends," Jordan scolded.

"Can I have my phone back please?"

"Why?"

"So, I can call my mother. I promise I'll leave Jackson alone for tonight."

We weren't officially a couple, but he was mine as much as I tried to keep us apart. I refused to let Jackson walk away from what our future could become.

Chapter Twenty-Three

Jackson

"What did you say?"

"She's pregnant," Brent told me.

The glass slipped out of my hand. Brent stepped forward to help, and I waved him off and sat on the couch.

"Pregnant?" I muttered to myself.

"Yep. She's been held up at the house in the country, resting and away from stress. Sorry, Jackson. I thought you should know."

"Is the baby mine?"

"Jackson, we both know that it couldn't be anyone else's. I understand you're pissed about her lying, but it's your baby."

"Why are you defending her?"

"Look, you both need to hash out your problems together. All of this back and forth arguing and bringing other people into your business is not helping anything."

"I need some space. Can you let yourself out?"

"Does she know you're here?"

"Yeah. I told her when I left the house, I was coming straight here. She's out in the car, waiting to come inside."

"I thought you said she didn't need to be around stress?"

"That's true, but you both need to come to terms with what's happening in your relationship. A baby's about to be born, and you can't start off with the parents hating each other."

Hearing the doorbell go off, Brent went to answer it, and Emery stood on the other side with a swollen belly. Her skin was glowing, and she'd put on some weight in her hips and breasts. From the dress she wore, I could tell she loved the extra curves and bigger breasts.

If I weren't so pissed off about her hiding her pregnancy, I would fuck her right now on the couch. But with me finding out about her being sick and currently pregnant, avoiding her would be punishment enough.

"Hi."

She walked inside and stood right in front of me.

"Why?"

"I'm sorry for keeping you away and hiding my illness. I thought if I could push you away, it would mean less of a heartache for me when the time comes."

"Why didn't you tell me about the baby?"

Reaching out to rub her belly, I hesitated and stepped back. She grabbed my wrists and placed my hands on her stomach.

"Please forgive me, Jackson. Nothing is going on with Anthony; that's in the past. Keeping secrets wasn't about trust... it was about keeping you from getting hurt."

"Emery, I can handle whatever comes our way if we do it together. The problem is you think you don't need any help, sweetness. You have everything under control. We're meant to support and love each other through the ups and down. But I won't be made a fool of and disrespected. Lying and keeping your pregnancy away from me is wrong."

Brent started to leave, and I needed time alone with the news he just dropped.

"You can go with him."

"What, Jackson..." Emery stuttered as tears pooled into her eyes.

"Emery, give him some space," Brent said as he walked her out.

I slammed the door and leaned my back with my eyes closed in thought.

* * *

The next day

I couldn't let my personal life interrupt my professional business, and tonight was an example of me not getting caught up and missing out on events that furthered my company.

"Thank you so much for this prestigious honor. I not only speak for myself and the team that we've strived to bring entertainment to everyone who visits our field."

"Mr. Pierce, is it true you have a baby on the way?" a reporter asked as I stepped off the podium after my company won the NASCAR Indy 500 race.

"No comment."

We finished the season in high ranking for sports entertainment and won our first primary race. I guess you could say Townsend Advertisement put us on the map. This past month, traveling from coast to coast had been exhausting. Not hearing or seeing Emery was another cause of my exhaustion. I had spies that kept me updated on her progress with the baby.

Brent made her take early maternity leave, and her family and friends kept me in the loop. I still couldn't come to grips with her holding so much in the dark about her illness. She wanted to always be in control, and now her stubbornness had us both miserable.

I was driving to meet Brent for an early celebration lunch. He wanted to have it at his place. Pulling up to his house four blocks over from my home, I loosened my tie and got out of my car to walk inside. Seeing all the cars here had me thinking he was probably throwing a celebration party. Something I wasn't in the mood for after dealing with a bunch of reporters all day.

The door was open, so I let myself inside and noticed coworkers, family, and friends sitting around, drinking.

"Surprise!" everyone yelled.

"Ohh, shoot. I thought we had enough time to turn off the lights and hide," Lauren said.

Brent walked up to shake my hand, and I saw Angela roll her eyes at Lauren. Jordan was feeding DJ on the couch. I knew Emery would be here, and I was nervous being in the same room with her. I wondered if she still had a hold on my heart.

"Don't worry, Jackson; she's not here. She did say congrats on everything. I thought it was best she stayed home," Brent said.

"How is she doing?"

Shrugging his shoulders in response, Brent passed me a beer, and I took a sip, waiting to see if Emery would pop out of a closet or room. I'd swoop her up and take her far away from here.

"I can see you've forgiven her. Have you said those words to her yet?" Brent asked.

Not wanting to mess up his party, I waved off his comment and went to greet his guests.

The party finally ended around ten, and somehow, I was outside Emery's new house in her parking space. I found out she'd moved into a new home, away from the drama with Anthony. Seeing the lights off, I contemplated if I should go or stay before removing the key and getting out.

Ten minutes after knocking, I heard the locks turn, and the door opened. Emery stood right in front of me with a round belly, tight shorts clinging to her thick hips, and a thin string bikini t-shirt, showing her normal-size breasts had tripled in size. Licking my lips, I adjusted my pants, so she didn't see my dick trying to spring out.

"Can I come inside?"

She moved to the side as I walked inside and closed the door behind me.

"What are you doing here, Jackson?"

"I don't know, Emery. A part of me wants to just turn around and never look back, and another part wants to take you upstairs and make love to you all night long," I responded and sat across from her on the couch.

"I take it you've been in contact with Brent."

"He's kept tabs on you for me, and of course, Granny Lynn always calls and reminds me that since I laid with you, I'm stuck with her for the rest of my life since we're having a baby together."

She looked nervous at my comment.

"I'm sorry, it was never my intention to keep you away from your child. Things between us happened so fast and then both our exes and my illness."

"Why did you hide it from your family?"

"Because I didn't want to believe I was sick. All of my life I was fine and worked hard. I pushed myself to be the best and go after the next goal in life; I never needed help. Anthony cheated, and then I remembered how sick my grandfather was when I was younger. Something clicked in my mind that if I didn't acknowledge it or tell anyone, then it wasn't true. Not putting my family through that, I felt, was for the best."

"How are things with your family now?"

"They've forgiven me and help me manage things better. Why are you here, Jackson? Have you forgiven me?"

Standing and helping Emery off the couch, I wiped the tears from her eyes. Smiling at her nervousness, I bent down, grazed my tongue across her top lip, and coaxed my tongue into her waiting mouth.

"I've missed you so much," I said as I ran my hand up and down her back.

"I've missed you too, Mr. Pierce."

"We still have a lot to talk about, but for right now. let's go upstairs. I've missed being inside you, sweetness."

Weeks later, Emery and I had dinner with Brent and her family and friends.

"How are you feeling, Emery?" Granny Lynn asked

"A little tired, but Jackson's helping me, Granny. I still have a little work to catch up on, and Brent's letting me slowly handle a few things," she said.

"Are you happy about being a father, Jackson? I know

it was hard dealing with Emery's stubbornness. She gets it from her grandfather," Granny Lynn said.

Everyone laughed at her comment, and Emery rolled her eyes and bit her top lip to avoid me peering at her.

"I won't lie, Granny, it took me a while to adjust to learning I'm a father, and then to find out from someone other than Emery. The hardest thing would have to be her keeping her diagnosis to herself. As you know, from our first meeting at Sybil's, Emery and I had a connection and started seeing each other, and something about her made me fall deeper and deeper in love."

"It was probably her sex. She gets it from my side of the family," Granny Lynn said.

Emery buried her face into her hands and groaned in frustration while everyone at the table laughed.

"Well, I won't complain, and I thank you and—"

"Jackson!" Emery shrieked out.

"Don't get quiet now. Emery, you better let that man worship you and let them tramps in New York realize he's locked down."

"Granny, please move on from talking about my sex life," Emery said as the waitress placed our food down on the table.

"As I was saying, we've talked and are in a better space now. Emery knows that what she did not only affected her family and me, but our baby as well. At the end of the day, it's not about her having control, but making sure she has a healthy pregnancy. "

Looking down at the future mother of my kids, we kissed, and she wiped the lipstick off my lips. We continued to laugh and joke with her family and friends.

Chapter Twenty-Four

Days later.

Standing in front of the mirror as Angela's assistant placed the veil over my head, I thought back to the day the doctor diagnosed me with lupus. I felt that my life was over at such a young age. Sticking with my medication especially while being pregnant was an extra caution that Jackson had taken on himself.

Angela and Jordan wanted to take me on a bachelorette trip, and Jackson vetoed that immediately. After begging and plenty of oral pleasure, he caved as long as I checked in with the doctor in the city and brought along bodyguards.

"Wow... Emery, you look so beautiful," Mom said as she walked inside our bridal room.

"Has everyone arrived yet?"

"Yes. Why did you agree to let Anthony come?"

"A wise man once told me I needed to let go of the hurt. At one point in time, Anthony played a big part in my life even before we dated. Hating Anthony for so long allowed him to have power over my emotions, and Jackson opened my eyes to what true love can do."

"I see you've been talking with your grandfather."

Looking over my shoulder, I gave her a knowing smile, acknowledging her statement.

"Yep. These past few months have shown me that my life was at a standstill. The constant back and forth with Jackson and hiding what was going on with my health didn't help either."

"All done, Emery," Anna said and stood to the side, so I could see the full look.

"Anna, you outdid yourself. Where's Jordan and Angela?"

"Making sure everything is set up for you in the church and reception hall," Anna replied and packed her makeup away.

"Anna, let the coordinator know I'm ready."

Hearing the bells chime and the music play, I saw my father walk in, ready to escort me out.

"We better hurry up and get you front and center before your future husband comes to kidnap you."

Sliding my arm inside my father's, I grabbed the bouquet from Anna and allowed her and my mom to walk ahead of me. Standing at the entrance, I could see inside and all my family and friends, including Anthony with his daughter. Can you believe it? Teresa up and left him for someone else? Not surprised at all, since she thought stealing Anthony would break me. I ended up winning something even better in the end. The doors opened, and all the anger, sadness, and loss I'd felt over the separation with Jackson faded away.

The love of my life, the one constant person who had never given up, even though I pushed him away, was waiting for me. Gripping my father's arm tightly, we walked down the aisle as everyone smiled and took pictures.

"He's good for you," Dad whispered in my ear as he placed my hand into Jackson's.

"Who here gives this woman away?" the pastor asked.

"My wife and I," Dad replied.

I looked up into Jackson's face and saw a small tear running down. Brent handed a handkerchief toward him.

"You look beautiful, sweetness," Jackson saw as he held my hand up to his lips for a kiss.

"Thank you, Mr. Pierce."

Two hours later, we walked into our reception to a Beyoncé song Hello, one of my favorites.

"Introducing Mr. & Mrs. Jackson Pierce!" the deejay yelled out through the microphone.

As we walked through the crowds, greeting our guests, Jackson held onto me protectively, not once letting my hand go.

"Baby, how long do we have to be here?"

"Jackson, we just got married. I want to mingle with our guests for a little while. You'll have me all to yourself tonight."

"Baby, come on... just a little quickie in the room. I'll be fast."

"Now, you know you, and a quickie never works out that way. That's why I'm pregnant now. Sorry, baby, you have to wait. How about we sit in our seats and do the speeches and toast?"

Agreeing with my request, we headed to the main table for the bride and groom with the rest of the wedding party. I noticed Angela and Brent standing at the mic. I was a little nervous about what would come out of her mouth.

"Jordan, has Angela and Brent behaved themselves tonight?"

Watching her finish one champagne glass with two more glasses empty in front of her, I wondered if something was bothering her. Following her line of sight, I saw Brent's friend Damon huddled at a table with a woman, with his arm around the back of her chair.

"How many drinks have you had, Jordan?"

"Not enough."

"You should talk to him. It's time you moved on and started a new relationship, J."

She folded her arms and pouted, looking just like her son DJ whenever he didn't get his way.

"Fuck him. Besides, tonight is about you and Jackson," she slurred and picked up another glass of champagne. I took it out of her hands and motioned for the waiter to bring her some water.

"You've had enough for tonight. Anyway, if Damon catches you drunk, he'll probably curse you and me out. Where's DJ?" Looking around the room, she pointed to him playing with Damon's daughter Tessa and some other kids, standing close to her father and his date.

"Well, if you want the man, you better step up to the plate and fight for him."

Turned toward me with a scowl on her face, she snorted under her breath and tried to stand to leave. Pulling her back down, I pointed toward Angela and Brent arguing at the other end of the table, and we both burst into laughter. Angela yanked the microphone out of his hand and cleared her throat to start her speech.

"Emery, we've been friends for many years. I call you

my sister, not just a friend. You and the Stone family saved my life when I came to live with your family. Jackson, when you walked up to her that day in Sybil's, I knew you'd be the one for her. No one has ever tamed that cold heart of hers."

"Whatever," I responded.

"I'm kidding, bestie, but for real, Jackson, take care of her, or you're going to have to see me. I'd hate to mess up your handsome face."

Everyone in the room laughed, and Jackson just shook his head with a side smile. All night, we danced and listened to people give speeches and offer congratulations.

Watching my grandmother and grandfather dancing with my little cousin, and DJ learning all the new moves, made my heart swell with joy. I was genuinely thankful that I could trust in Jackson's love, knowing he never wavered even when I wanted to let him go and have a life with someone who didn't have any baggage.

He placed a gentle kiss on my cheek and rubbed my growing belly.

"How are you feeling?"

"Babe, my feet are swollen, and I'm ready to lie with you wrapped around me. How much longer is this going to take?" I asked, annoyed and picking at my food as Jackson took off my heels and rubbed my feet.

"Sweetness, let your family enjoy this time while they can. Soon as our little one gets here, you know we'll both be too busy to even go to family dinners. Just relax and calm down."

Reaching out to grab his hands, I raised them to my lips and placed a kiss on both of his palms.

"Are you sure we can't sneak out for a little bit?"

Smirking at my attempt to seduce him, Jackson

leaned over and kissed me on the lips, forehead, and chin. Knowing my hormones were crazy, he coaxed my mouth further with his tongue.

"You don't play fair, Jackson."

"Sorry, baby. I'll try to behave myself a little while longer."

"Yeah, right."

We both burst out into laughter and looked over at Angela and Brent arguing near the podium.

"Those two are such a mess."

"That's your friend, playing my boy. Now's he's stuck in a miserable relationship because of Angela's games."

"I know she's stubborn, and I've tried to get her to let her walls down and tell him how she feels. Angela's gone through a lot, and her trust has been broken so much from her parents abandoning her or by trifling men."

"Tonight is all about you and our future life as Mr. and Mrs. Pierce. Leave all the other drama alone and focus on my baby growing and your health."

"I promise to focus on our family going forward and not keeping you out of the loop. I apologize again for not telling you about my pregnancy. I was childish and wrong."

Squeezing my hand in comfort, Jackson stared intensely into my eyes, pulled me up from my seat, and placed me into his lap.

"Emery, I love you, and nothing will take you away from me. I promise to fight all your battles with you, but you have to let me in, baby."

"Deal."

We both smiled as we looked out at our family and friends joking and having fun.

Chapter Twenty-Five

Jackson

Thinking back over the past few months since meeting Emery at the restaurant, I knew we were in a place of just wanting to forget. The choice to continue pursuing her and getting my heart stomped on wasn't in my plans at the beginning. Something kept bringing me back to her. Between her secret about her health and finding out she was hiding her pregnancy nearly tore us apart.

Remembering back on our many nights of throwing caution to the wind, it was bound to happen. Knowing Emery wanted to hide her pregnancy was the last straw. No matter what our issues were, she shouldn't have kept my son away from me. The moment she found out she was pregnant, I should have been the first call. Luckily, Brent visited her while she was resting at her home in Martha's Vineyard. The day we got married she promised to never keep another secret from me again.

Lounging on the beach on Honeymoon Island off the coast of Fiji with the sun rays kissing her skin, I looked at her growing belly bump. Realizing how I could have lost her made my chest tighten. Pulling her closer, we continued listening to the waves against the beach.

"How are you feeling, sweetness?"

She let out an exasperated sigh. "Babe, come on, you said no talking about my condition. If you haven't noticed, we're on our honeymoon. Focus on making love to me instead."

Letting go of some of the tension, I pressed my lips to the side of her cheek, under her ear, hitting her spot.

"Woman, you drive me crazy, you know that? Fine, I won't bring it up again if you do one favor for me?" Casting a sneaky grin, I helped her to sit across my lap with her six-month belly separating us.

"What's this for, Mr. Pierce?"

Rubbing around her belly and feeling my son moving around made my heart swell even more. After the breakup with Jessica, getting married never crossed my mind.

"I would love if you'd do me the honor of marrying me every year for the next hundred years."

She slipped her hand in my swim trunks and took out my dick. She squeezed gently, and I grunted from the pain and pleasure she placed on my body. Loosening her top, her breasts fell out. Licking my lips, ready to attack, I scooted her back a little as I moved forward to capture her nipple in my mouth.

"Jackson... Mmmmm... When's the staff coming again?"

Moving her bikini bottom to the side, she lifted a little as I placed my cock at her center. I buried myself as deep as possible into her wet core. Her juices buried my cock as we slowly rocked back and forth, and I tasted her dark-tipped nipples that reminded me of a chocolate Hershey's kiss drop. She crossed her hands around my neck and arched her back, quickening her pace.

"Goddamn... Emery."

Gripping her hips, we moved in sync, and she sucked me in further. Smelling her arousal, I ran a finger down to her most sensitive place.

"I'm sorry for waiting so late to love you," Emery whispered as she pulled my face closer to her waiting lips.

"I'd wait forever for you, baby."

Picking her up in my arms by her butt, we switched positions, and I laid her on her back while still inside her.

"Arghhh, yes... Jackson."

"Fuckkk... sweetness," I bellowed out as she locked her legs around my back and pulled me in closer, stroking my back. Not wanting to hurt the baby, I made sure to keep a little distance between us as my movements picked up. I pounded at her core. Having the luxury of owning an island came in handy.

"Please, oh God. Yesssss." Emery screamed as her orgasm took over, and I kept a steady rhythm with my thrusts. Feeling dizzy and lightheaded with sweat dripping off my brow. The pressure of my semen at the tip of my dick seeped into her walls. I couldn't stop coming.

"Shittt... Argh. Fuck!"

With shaky legs, I tried to avoid falling on top of her. I gained some strength to pull out and drop in the chair next to her. Out of breath, I grabbed her hand and placed a kiss on top. She moved in closer and laid her head on my chest.

"Jackson, you own my heart."

"To think when we first met, you were stone cold against letting anyone get close to you, and now you're married and pregnant with my baby."

"It seems your heart was big enough for the both of us."

* * *

I hope you enjoyed Emery and Jackson's story so far. Check out **Heart of Stone Book 1.5** at my shop https://payhip.com/b/kWg7

Are you interested in Mafia romance? Check into *Antonio & Sabrina: Struck in Love, Books 1* https://book s2read.com/u/4AxKLo

Follow **Heart of Stone Book 2 Jordan and Damon** https://books2read.com/u/ba2OMx

Follow a Second chance romance here "H**eart of Stone Book 3 Angela and Brent"** https://book s2read.com/u/31rx9l

Get into a One night stand romance with **Jessica and Joseph**

Heart of Stone Book 3.5 https://payhip.com/ b/HGP1

Heart of Stone Book 4 Jessica and Joseph https://books2read.com/u/4NXyPG

If you want more "Mafia Romance, why not try *"Antonio and Sabrina Book 2" Click here* https://books2read.com/u/bpED6g

Have you read *yet* **"Temptation?** That is a stand-alone contemporary, sports, curvy girl romance. Check it out here https://books2read.com/u/mle1Vv

* * *

Check out **Aydin a grumpy boss, bodyguard romance** here https://books2read.com/u/mBwaOy .Follow my standalone opposites attract, age gap, military romance "**Exposed**" https://books2read.com/u/bQyYZe .

Are you a fan of sports romance? Then download one-night stand, billionaire romance "**Refuel**" https://books2read.com/u/boDyDA. Also, follow it up with workplace, sports romance "**Pressure**" https://books2read.com/u/3Ly1r7 .

If you love romantic comedy, fake relationships, enemies to lovers, find it here, "**Something Gained.**" Click the link https://books2read.com/u/baGLYy .

Any fan of forbidden romance, political? Check out "**Mutual Agreement**" https://books2read.-com/u/mgzzWX a steamy romance. Pre-order the full novel of "**Nasir**" here click the link here.

Have you checked out "**She's All I Need**" click here https://books2read.com/u/49lkeW a sports, opposites attract romance. What about dark romance that has everything from steamy romance, opposites attract, suspense, thriller, celebrity, and more "**Joaquin Fuertes Book 1**" https://books2read.com/u/mvZlgV

Catch up with favorite characters in this holiday short romance which includes spoilers. https://books2read.com/u/bzd59G

Playlist

Heart of Stone Book 1 (Emery & Jackson)

1. Janet Jackson (Go Deep)
2. Maxwell (Til the Cops Come Knockin)
3. Whitney Houston (You Give Good Love)
4. Jill Scott (He Loves Me)
5. Beyonce (Rocket)
6. Beyonce (Mine)
7. Adele (Someone Like You)
8. Mario (Let Me Love You)
9. Carl Carlton (She's A Bad Mama Jama
10. Faith Hill (Breathe)
11. Alicia Keys (Fire We Make)
12. Kelly Clarkson (Love So Soft)
13. Joe (All The Things Your Man Won't Do)

Reader Questions:

Email responses to <u>info@304publishing.com</u>

    1. Do you think Angela's really pregnant?

    2. Do you think Granny should cut Pop's a break?

    3. Should Emery and Jackson set boundaries for family and friends?

Heart of Stone series

Heart of Stone Book 1 Emery and Jackson
https://books2read.com/u/boWPAV
Heart of Stone Book 1.5
https://payhip.com/b/kWg7
Heart of Stone Book 2 Jordan and Damon
https://books2read.com/u/ba2OMx
Heart of Stone Book 3.5 Bottoms Up
https://payhip.com/b/HGP1
Heart of Stone Book 3 Angela and Brent
https://books2read.com/u/31rx9l
Heart of Stone Book 4 Jessica and Joseph
https://books2read.com/u/4NXyPG

Antonio and Sabrina Series

Order of Reading

The Early Years-A Prequel Short Story
https://books2read.com/u/49Zjnw
Ruthless Struck In Love Book 1
https://books2read.com/u/4AxKLo
Savage Struck In Love Book 2
https://books2read.com/u/bpED6g
Beast Struck In Love Book 3
https://books2read.com/u/3LpgdJ
Janice and Carlo Captivated By His Love
https://books2read.com/u/b6je6M
Brutal Struck In Love Book 4
https://books2read.com/u/4NQyE9
Stolen-Fuertes Mafia Cartel Book 1
https://books2read.com/u/mvZlgV
Saved-Fuertes Mafia Cartel Book 2
https://books2read.com/u/4DWwLd
Redemption Struck In Love Book 5
https://books2read.com/u/b5kZ8O

Betrayal- Fuertes Mafia Cartel Book 3
https://books2read.com/u/4A5LGp

Catalogue of Releases

The Early Years-A Prequel Short Story
    Struck in Love 1, 2, 3,4,5
    Heart of Stone, Book 1 (Emery & Jackson)
    Heart Of Stone Book 1.5 Emery &Jackson A Valentine's Day Short
    Janice and Carlo: Captivated By His Love
    Heart of Stone, Book 2 (Jordan and Damon)
    Temptation
    Heart of Stone, Book 3 (Angela and Brent)
    Bottoms Up Heart of Stone, Book 3.5(Jessica and Joseph Short
    Cocky Catcher
    Bossy Billionaire
    Love Shorts:A Collection of Short Stories
    Stolen Fuertes Mafia Cartel Book 1
    Saved Fuertes Mafia Cartel Book 2
    Exposed (Salvation Society Novel)
    Betrayal Fuertes Mafia Cartel Book 3
    Refuel(A Driven World Novel)
    Pressure(A Driven World Novel)

Until Serena(HEA World Novel)
Exposed (Salvation Society Novel)
Heart of Stone, Book 4 (Jessica and Joseph)
She's All I Need
Something Gained (Romantic Comedy)
Thank you so much for reading, and if you enjoyed the crazy ride and decide to leave a review, we'd truly appreciate the support.

What's Next

Want to know what happens next?

Follow me on my website to catch the next release.

Reviews are the lifeblood of the publishing world. They're read, appreciated, and needed.

Please consider taking the time to leave a few words on your review platform of choice.

Sign up for updates and sneak peaks at the site below. www.chiquitadennie.com

304 Publishing Company

The home of authors African American, Interracial, Women's Fiction, Fantasy, Erotic, and Contemporary Romance novels. Along with Thriller, Suspense, Poetry, Beauty, and Style Books. Thank you for taking the time out to visit. Join our mailing list to stay updated with new releases and blog posts.

Acknowledgments

I want to dedicate this to my team that helps me behind the scenes, from my editors, test readers, graphic designers, and the list goes on. Truly appreciate each of you for keeping me on my toes.

About the Author

Chiquita Dennie is an author of Contemporary, Romantic Suspense, Erotic, Thriller, Mystery, and Women's Fiction. Chiquita lives in Los Angeles, CA. Before she started writing contemporary romance, she worked in the entertainment industry on notable TV shows such as The Dr Phil Show, The Tyra Banks Show, American Idol, and Deal or No Deal. But her favorite job is the one she's now doing full time: writing romance.

A best-selling author and award-winning filmmaker, her first short film Invisible was released in summer 2017 and screened in multiple festivals and won for Best Short Film. Also, she hosts a podcast that showcases the latest in beauty, business, and community called "Moscato and Tea." Her debut release of Antonio and Sabrina Struck In Love has opened a new avenue of writing that she loves.

If you want to know when the next book will come out, please visit her website at http://www.chiquitaden nie.com, where you can sign up to receive an email for her next release.